"Was I a better lover than Paul?"

A muscle moved in Luke's jaw as he asked the question.

Kim didn't hesitate. It was a reflex action, born of humiliation. She threw the coffee at her husband and with a faint, ghastly feeling inside of her watched it pour down his face and sweater.

Luke moved like lightning to shake her. She had never seen anyone so angry. When he spoke, his voice was low and controlled with fury. "You'll be sorry you did that," he said, and flung her away from him.

"I won't let you touch me again," she hissed.

"Won't you? I wouldn't be too sure of that if I were you." His smile chilled her blood. Luke was bent on punishing her, and there wasn't a thing she could do about it!

Other titles by

# MARY WIBBERLEY
## IN HARLEQUIN PRESENTS

Other titles by

# MARY WIBBERLEY
## IN HARLEQUIN ROMANCES

# MARY WIBBERLEY

## savage love

*Harlequin Books*

TORONTO·LONDON·NEW YORK·AMSTERDAM
SYDNEY·HAMBURG·PARIS·STOCKHOLM

Harlequin Presents edition published March 1980
ISBN 0-373-10348-4

Original hardcover edition published in 1978
by Mills & Boon Limited

# CHAPTER ONE

KIM had heard the scream of brakes even above the rolling of the thunder—a blinding, grinding shifting of balance—and then stillness.

'Wait,' said the man. 'Wait, don't try to move.' She opened her eyes again to see him, and knew she must be dreaming. The car was at a crazy angle, and her seat belt held her firmly wedged behind the wheel, and the man's hands were busy as he sought to release her. But it wasn't his hands she watched, it was his face. She had recognised his voice, and thought she was mad. There was no mistaking that lean dark face bending over her, not looking at her, concentrating only on freeing her from the prison of her car. And all the while the thunder rolled and the lightning flashed around them, and in one of the flashes she saw him so clearly that her heart stopped for an instant.

Luke Savage, her ex-husband. The man who had made her so desperately unhappy, three years previously, that for a time life had become a grey, barren waste. Then she had got over it, painfully; inch by inch she had crawled back to life—and now suddenly, on a remote road in the wilds of Westmorland, as if at the hands of some malignant fate, she had crashed her car into his.

Overtaking him, the storm at its height, lightning

zigzagging around the hills, and a sheep suddenly
panicking and trying to cross then changing its mind—
then the screech of brakes, the grinding of metal—and
a brief oblivion.

He was drenched with the rain that lashed down
into the side-turned car. She could feel it on her face
as well, icy cold, reviving her by the minute. Which
was when she started to struggle. 'No—leave me
alone——' He must have thought she was hysterical.
For she knew in a moment of instinct that he hadn't
recognised her—yet. Or perhaps he had simply forgotten. And which was worse?

'You're safe,' his voice was soothing. Kim had never
heard him speak soothingly before. It wasn't in character. He was tough, abrasive—and yet. . . . 'The seat belt
saved you from going through the windscreen, but it's
jammed. Ah—no, that's it.' She was free, free to move.
To see him, to face him. Any moment she would see
the look in his eyes, see the sympathy change to shock.
But it didn't. He picked her up and carried her over
to his own car which waited on the road with its boot
dented severely.

'Get in.' He deposited her in the passenger seat and
she lay back, suffering from shock. Not the kind he
imagined—but the shock only of seeing him. For she
was unhurt, she knew that.

'I'll get your luggage out of your car. Stay there. I'll
take you to where you're going—you understand me?'

'Yes,' she whispered. When he had gone she leaned
over and looked at herself in the rear view mirror, and
knew one good reason why he might not have recog-

nised her. Her face was smeared with blood.

She reached up to touch, to find the cut on her forehead—and his voice came: 'Don't do that. It's a flesh wound, not deep. I've got your cases, and I've locked your car—what's left of it. It's not blocking the road —now, where are you going?'

Then he turned to her, and he was holding a white handkerchief, soaked with water. 'Rain,' he said. 'Wipe your face—gently now. Or shall I do it?' He still didn't know.

'Thanks, I will.' She began to dab carefully at her cheeks and chin. It was dark outside, and he switched on the interior light, and then, in that hush that followed, she sensed the sudden withdrawal, the shock.

'My God,' he said. 'You!'

She looked at him. She was already over the worst, but he had gone white. For an instant she thought she glimpsed hatred in his eyes, then it vanished and it might have been her imagination. To her dismay she found she was trembling. 'Yes, it's me.' She had to force herself to breathe more calmly. 'It's all right. If you'll just drop me at the next village, I'll——'

'Where are you going?' he said again, and the tone was noticeably different from before.

'To the Rykin Hotel. It's about ten——'

'I know where it is.' He gripped the steering wheel until his knuckles showed white. 'Why? Why are you going there?'

She didn't understand him. 'I don't see——' she began, but he cut in:

'Why there? You couldn't possibly have known——'

'It belongs to my cousin. I'm going to help her.'

Luke turned on her, eyes blazing. She saw him as she had never seen him before, in those blissful weeks, so many years ago.... 'You liar!' he snapped. There was such force and power in his words, in the way they were said, and the car seemed as storm-filled as the very air outside, as if the electrical impulses were within, and Kim put her hand to her cheek and stared helplessly at him, shaken and frightened. There was leashed violence within him, a strength and anger she neither understood nor could withstand. She wanted only to get away, to escape the dreadful anguish which filled her. Tugging at the handle of the door, she opened it—but his hand clamped down over hers, and pulled her back.

'Don't be a fool,' he grated.

'No! Leave me—don't touch me——' she began, struggling, terrified. Weakly she fell back against the seat, eyes wide and shocked. Luke leaned over and locked the door.

'I'm not going to hurt you,' he said harshly. 'Did you think I was? My God, I'd like to—but I'm not going to. Sit still.'

'I'm not a liar,' she burst out. 'It's true. My cousin Emma Devlin runs the hotel, and her husband's ill, and I'm going there——'

He looked at her. 'And so am I,' he answered grimly. 'But if I'd known you were, I'd not have gone within a thousand miles of the place.' Then he started the car, and he neither looked at her nor did he speak, as with a roar they set off down the road.

The rest of the journey was a nightmare, there was no other way to describe it. The ten miles were accomplished at speed, and the concentration needed on Luke's part was sufficient to leave Kim time to collect her scattered thoughts. The scenery passed in a blur of speed and rain, accompanied by lightning and rolling thunder. She clung to her seat for dear life, her mind in a turmoil. He was going there, *he* was going too. It was like a bad dream. Higher and higher they climbed, into the hills, driving along narrow roads surrounded by trees, and no other cars, nothing save the two of them, together and yet not together, for it was as if a wall of silence and dislike separated them.

As they saw the long grey stone building in the distance, briefly hidden by trees and then visible again, she found her voice and her courage.

'Why did you call me a liar?' she asked. 'Did you think I knew you'd be there?' She looked at the hard profile beside her. 'Did you think I'd have gone if I'd known?'

Luke stopped the car, there on a bend near the entrance to the driveway, and turned to her. 'If you feel as I do—no,' he replied.

'Then why—why are you coming?'

His face changed slightly. 'Because once—once— this place had something that drew me to it. It was a long time ago.' His voice was harsh again. 'And nothing to do with you.' His eyes raked her face, her body.

'You are nothing to me now. Do you understand?'

'I always did,' she answered quietly. 'Oh yes, I understand all right. The past is dead and gone.' For an instant she turned away to look out of the window lest he see the sudden tears that brimmed over. 'And you are nothing to me. We're strangers—perhaps we always were.' She blinked a few times, then turned to face him again. 'And always will be,' she added softly.

'As long as we both remember that.' He turned the ignition key and the noise of the engine filled the car again. Then he turned into the drive, and Kim felt her fists clench helplessly. He made himself very clear. She didn't know how long he intended to stay at the Rykin, she hoped it would be brief, but however many—or few—days, she would cope. She had done so before. He wasn't going to ruin her life again.

Emma's concern washed over Kim in a warm tide of mingled affection and worry. Kim sat on the bed in her small attic room, and Emma carefully applied the plaster to her forehead and stood back to survey her handiwork.

'There,' she said, 'that'll be all right. Now are you sure you don't want to lie down for a while?'

Kim smiled up at her. 'No, I'm fine, honestly,' she lied. Physically she was, it was only the other, inner thoughts that confused. And Emma had never known about Luke, which was a relief. Their marriage had been secret—and brief.

'Good. Then we'll go down. It was very kind of Mr Savage to bring you—though he was coming anyway,' she laughed merrily. 'What a coincidence, though!'

'Wasn't it just?' murmured Kim.

'And such a good-looking man—though he looks as though he has too many late nights—a bit—what's the word?' she frowned.

'Dissipated?' suggested Kim wryly.

'Mm, no, not exactly—more—oh, I don't know. He looks as though he could do with a good rest anyway.' Kim did not want to talk about Luke Savage, she quite definitely did not, but Emma clearly did.

'But he'll get one here. That's the one thing we can guarantee at this place—peace and quiet.' She smiled at Kim fondly. 'You look as though you could do with a holiday yourself, instead of slaving here for me——'

'Slaving?' Kim laughed. 'I'd hardly call helping you for a couple of weeks slaving. It'll be fun.' Or would be if he wasn't here. . . .

'I'll enjoy having you. There's so much to talk about, and it's so lonely with Bill in hospital, and the kids away at Aunt Jessie's for the holidays——'

'How is Bill?' asked Kim.

'Going on nicely. But he'll be in a while——'

'How often can you visit?'

'Now you're here I can probably manage twice a week. Mr and Mrs Barnes are very good but, you know how it is, I like to be here to greet people and answer the phone——' Emma paused.

'Well, you can stop worrying about it now I'm here,' Kim said firmly. 'Because I'll take over all that. You just concentrate on your wonderful cooking.' She grimaced at her dirty hands. 'Talking of which, I'm starving! If you'll just let me have a good wash I'll be down in two minutes.'

'Watch your forehead, near the hairline. Don't disturb the plaster.'

'I won't.' Kim realised something that had simply not occurred to her before. 'Er—he wasn't hurt at all, was he?'

'Mr Savage?' Emma looked puzzled for a moment. 'He never said—and I was so concerned about you I never thought to ask.' She put her hand to her face. 'I'd better go and see. His room's below this one. Come to think of it, he did look a bit shaken. More as if he'd had a shock than anything else.' She went out, closing the door softly behind her.

A shock. Kim walked to the washbasin in the corner and ran the taps, looking at herself in the mirror as she did so. Yes, he'd had a shock all right. And so have I, she thought, seeing her face, still white and pale in the aftermath of all that had happened. It is a shock to see a man you once thought you loved—especially when he's pulling you out of a wrecked car—a man you hoped never to see again, because it was all in the past, dead and buried like all lost loves should be. There was no going back, could never be, and shortly after it had happened, and the marriage had gone so explosively wrong, she had wished she had never met him. Now, with the years between to soften everything, she knew differently. We're changed by all our experiences, she thought. We're changed by all that happens to us, and in a way I'm a different person for having known him, for having shared, however briefly, something that was so unutterably wonderful at the time that I suppose I knew it couldn't last. The love I had for him—and thought he had for me—was like a flame lighting the world. She looked down at the water in the basin, and plunged her hands in it, as if to wash the bittersweet memories away.

He'll see me as I am now, she thought, as she gently washed her face. He'll see me, and he'll know that I was never his, because that's how I want it to be now. And when he leaves here, and we look at each other for the last time, he'll go away, and he'll remember only that I am as I am now—and he'll never know the pain he caused me three years ago.

She dried her face, combed her thick chestnut hair back, picked up her handbag, and went out of the room. Then, as she went down the last few stairs to the first floor, Luke was coming towards her from his room. Kim caught her breath, not prepared for the encounter. He had changed from the clothes he had been wearing —which had got soaked—into a white polo-necked sweater and grey slacks. He was as tall as she remembered, but broader-shouldered, his black hair flecked with grey at the temples. He looked at her with those hard blue-grey eyes that had once gazed at her so differently and said:

'Are you better now?' Not as if he cared, but as if manners forced it from him.

'Yes, thank you.' He was freshly washed and shaved too. His face was pale, so that his beard showed darkly on the white skin. She had teased him about that, called him 'Bluebeard' once, so many lifetimes ago, when everything had been wonderful, and his response had been to kiss her, to growl and say: 'But isn't that what you women like?' She shivered at the memory. He looked as if he had not seen enough sun lately. She wondered what he did for a living now, but would never ask. She didn't care.

'I think my cousin will have your meal ready in the dining room,' she said, as she began to go down the broad, red-carpeted staircase. 'Shall I show you where it is?'

'I'll find it. I telephoned the local garage while you were upstairs,' he told her, 'to go and tow your car in.'

Kim felt frankly surprised. 'That was—kind of you. I would have done it later.'

'I'm sure you would. But it's getting dark—it seemed safer to do it now. You'd had enough of a shock—it seemed the sensible thing to do.' He walked beside her, a head taller than Kim, a powerful animal whose strength she had known only too well—once—and yet now, had anyone watched them, they would have seemed like perfect strangers meeting briefly, talking politely on a staircase of a small hotel.

'Thank you.' At the bottom of the stairs, in the carpeted reception area, she turned to him. 'The dining room's over there. The dog's very old, and not a bit fierce. Her name's Fiona.' Then she walked away as Fiona, the aged black labrador, rose stiffly from where she had been stationed at the glass doors to the dining room, and waddled towards him. She heard, as she went towards the kitchen, Luke's voice as he spoke to the dog, and—she couldn't help it—she glanced briefly back to see him crouched down, stroking Fiona's head, while her long tail wagged slowly with pleasure.

Kim opened the door of the corridor that led to the kitchens, and closed it behind her. She would have to learn to be cool when they met. She would—she must —for her own peace of mind. But she would avoid him as much as possible.

Emma was busy with Mrs Barnes when she went in, and spared her only the briefest of glances. 'Sit down, love. Won't be a minute. There's three in for dinner tonight—no, four with our Mr Savage.' She was spooning vegetables on to plates, which the housekeeper then transferred to the dinner trolley, looking up and smiling at Kim in between doing so.

'Nice to see you, Kim. What a start to your visit, though, bumping your car. I make sure I stay indoors when a storm's on—frightened to death I am.' She was a plump white-haired woman whom Kim knew well, and liked. She and her husband had worked with Emma and Bill Devlin for the past six years, and she was nearly as good a cook as Emma, which was saying something.

Both women vanished, leaving Kim alone with her thoughts. She wondered who the other guests were. The hotel was so out of the way that passing, casual guests were almost unheard-of. But it had instead a regular clientele of annual visitors who came up for the peace and quiet, the walking, and birdwatching. Which made it all the more strange that someone like Luke should seek out this solitude. What was it he had said? 'Once this place had something that drew me to it—

a long time ago.' Then he had added, almost as if
making sure she would not—could not—possibly get
the wrong ideas: 'And nothing to do with you.' Had
he been there before they had met and married those
three long years ago? Emma and Bill had owned it for
seven. Or had he meant only the area? Kim felt confused and tired—not unnaturally, for she had driven
up from London since the morning, and the bump in
the car hadn't improved matters. I'll feel better and
think straighter, after an early night, she decided, and
told Emma so when at last her cousin was able to
snatch a moment to talk.

'Course you will, love,' agreed Emma. Kim knew
she was watching her as she ate the superb meal. She
thinks I don't eat enough, Kim supposed, accurately
enough, and she means to feed me up while I'm here
——'And if you keep serving food like this, I'll put on
a stone in no time,' she said out loud.

'Hmm, that won't do you any harm,' agreed Emma.
'Personally I don't hold with all this slimming business,' she patted her own plump hips complacently.

'Ah, but you've got Bill,' teased Kim, 'and anyway,'
with a brief glance down at her trim figure and neat
bosom, 'I'm not skinny—am I?'

'Course you're not,' Emma laughed. 'But still——'
she moved away from the table and went over to the
window, where rain lashed down ceaselessly outside.
'That Mr Savage now—*he* can eat, I can tell you——'
Kim tried to shut her ears to it. She didn't want to
know. 'He looks as if he could do with a few good meals
inside him as well.'

'Yes. When are you going to see Bill?' Kim interrupted desperately.

'Oh, tomorrow—now you're here. He hates being in hospital, you know—hates being inactive—but it's the only way, for the moment. They're considering fitting a pace-maker—sometimes it makes all the difference.' She turned again to Kim and her eyes had filled with tears. 'Do you think he'll be all right?'

'Of course he will.' Kim jumped up and went over to hug her. 'If that's what's needed, it'll do the trick, you'll see.'

'They're doing tests at the moment——' Emma stopped.

'You must go as often as you can,' Kim said reassuringly. 'That's the best heart medicine he can have—you'll soon have him home again. Why, lots of film stars and all sorts of active people have pace-makers fitted—and they lead perfectly normal lives——'

'But we might have to give up the hotel,' Emma interrupted. 'And we love it here so much.'

'But what's more important? Bill's health—or this place?'

Emma smiled. 'You're right, of course. Anyway, never mind us, how are the kids?'

'Well, let's say I always look forward to the holidays.' Kim grinned at her cousin. 'No, I love teaching, really. It's hard work, but it has its moments.' She sighed, seeing in her mind a picture of the school in a poorer part of London where she spent her weekdays teaching P.E. to primary school children of all races and colours. 'You could cry sometimes, and at others you could laugh—and then, one day, one of them does something that makes it all worth while.' She smiled, remembering. 'Only a week or so ago a little boy—only about seven, name of Thaddeus, and as black as coal, brought me a present, because he'd found out it was my birthday. He must have saved up all his money— it was a little vase, the brightest coloured thing you ever saw, all blues and reds and orange—and he'd wrapped it carefully in coloured tissue paper, and presented it to me, eyes shining, beaming all over his face.' She sighed. 'So I had him round to tea the following day with a couple of his friends—and you should have seen the expression on his face when he saw the little vase in the middle of my mantelpiece filled with anemones—I thought he'd burst with pride.'

Emma laughed. 'How marvellous! But you care, don't you? You really care?'

'Yes, I suppose I do. You can't teach if you don't. It shows through—and they know, and they respond. Some days I go home with a splitting headache—but I wouldn't swop my job for anything.' She shook her head.

'Not even if you met the right man?' asked Emma softly.

Kim drew breath. Some things, some memories— hurt, even after three years. 'Why,' she answered, with a lightness she didn't feel, 'how could I? *You've* already *got* Bill, haven't you?' And they both laughed.

But later Kim remembered their conversation. In the quietness of her room, high in the hotel, with the rain a soothing drumming on the window, and the darkness wrapping around her like a cloak, she remembered what had been—and she was filled with a sense of the sadness of life. And Luke was not far away, in the room below, but it might have been a million miles. She had not seen him again after dinner, she had made sure of that. With any luck, she might avoid him completely. She stood at the window, seeing herself reflected in the darkened glass, her cool serene face looking back at her, chestnut hair a blur, and there was nothing to tell her, no sense of precognition within her, just a quiet stillness to the air that gave her no warning of what was to come.

She turned away from the window and began to prepare for bed.

# CHAPTER TWO

KIM met the three other guests after breakfast the following morning, when she went in to help Emma clear away the plates. She was amused—but kept it well hidden—to find herself being coolly surveyed by two pairs of eyes, and rather more warmly observed by a third.

'Miss Dines and Mrs Beaumont,' said Emma pleasantly, 'I'd like you to meet my cousin Kim Sheridan who's come to assist me for a week or two.' She added helpfully, '*She's* a teacher as well.'

It was Miss Dines who spoke first. Clearly the leader of the two women, a magnificent figure who sat regally at the breakfast table, about fifty and with an attractive but hard face and extremely cold blue eyes, she nodded, 'How d'you do.' Those eyes missed nothing of Kim's appearance, and clearly were not too pleased with what they saw. 'My sister and I are here on a walking holiday—we come every year, don't we, Celia?' The faded shadow by her side nodded, clearly awaiting permission to speak before actually doing so. Kim wondered fleetingly what kind of school they taught at, and was willing to bet it was not a primary in the East End of London.

'And this is Colonel Pickering,' added Emma, turning away from the two schoolteachers. The Colonel rose gallantly to his feet and took Kim's hand. Large both in girth and height, and fiercely moustached, he nevertheless smiled warmly as he gave Kim a nutcracker handshake.

'Glad to meet you, m'dear,' he boomed. 'Lovely place this—just the background I need for what I'm doing?' He lowered his voice to just below boom level. 'Writing me memoirs, you see. Need peace an' quiet.'

'How fascinating,' said Kim, and kept, with difficulty, a warm and interested smile on her face.

'Yes, well,' said Emma brightly, coming neatly to the rescue. 'We'll let you finish your breakfast. More toast, Colonel—ladies?'

'No, thanks. Got to think of me figure,' roared the Colonel, and his laughter followed them from the room as they escaped, plate-laden, towards the kitchen. Safely inside, Emma collapsed against the table.

'Did you see them?' she giggled, as Mrs Barnes looked round interestedly from a bowl of soapy water. 'Weighing you up? I don't think Miss Dines cared for you too much——'

'I'll live,' shrugged Kim dryly. 'You could have warned me, though.'

'Oh no, it would have spoilt it,' gasped Emma, wiping a tear from her eye. 'She took a real shine to Mr Savage at dinner last night—I'll bet she thought—whooppee! and then she meets *you*!'

Kim could scarcely say anything. 'She's welcome to him' would not have been appropriate. 'Er—where do they teach?' she asked instead.

'Oh, some terribly posh boarding school in Bath,'

said Emma, recovering, 'and she's a crashing bore. Her sister's quite harmless—though she never says much.'

'I wouldn't think she'd dare,' responded Kim dryly. 'The Colonel seemed rather a sweetie.'

'He's been writing his memoirs for ten years—*ten years!*' said Emma, 'and comes here regularly every July. He's very gallant in that old-fashioned way——' she stopped and frowned. 'Why, Kim, what is it?'

Kim looked at her blankly. Because she had suddenly remembered, and it had all come rushing back into her mind at the mention of the word 'writing'. But she couldn't tell Emma. Not yet. Maybe not ever. She pulled herself together. 'What? Oh, sorry—nothing. I was just thinking what a monster Miss Dines must be——' she shivered. 'That poor sister!' She smiled at Emma. 'Well, thanks for introducing me. I wouldn't have missed it for anything. Now what's my first job today?'

And when she was vacuuming the dining room shortly afterwards, watched by Fiona, she allowed herself to think about Luke. Because now she remembered something that had, incredibly, gone completely from her mind for three years. Luke had been engaged on writing a book when she had first met him, and had been full of it, so full of enthusiasm that Kim had found herself caught up in his own excitement at the sheer joy he had found in putting words on paper. She wondered briefly if anything had ever become of it.

She sighed. What did it matter? She wished that certain words wouldn't trigger off memories of him. It was disturbing enough to have him in the same house.

One thing she had forgotten to ask Emma was how long he intended staying. And yet it might be better not to know at that. Then she mentally switched off all thoughts of him. It was something she had learned to do in those bitter months after their love had died —and now it would come in useful. He would see just how very controlled she was. She stood up straighter as she pushed the vacuum cleaner across the thick grey carpet, and deliberately made her expression cool and calm. If he should see....

'I'm sorry.' She whirled round, touching the vacuum switch as she did so, and it whizzed down into silence. He stood just inside the doorway, and Fiona lumbered across delightedly to him, wagging her tail.

'Yes?'

'I think I might have dropped my wallet.' He walked over to the window, followed by the dog. So he sat by the window, did he? Well away from the predatory Miss Dines. Kim wondered whose idea that had been.

'Ah yes, here it is.' Luke bent, picked something up, and straightened. He wore the same white polo-necked sweater, but now with matching jacket to the trousers over it, and the air in the room throbbed with invisible tension. Kim didn't speak, she merely waited for him to go. Neither patiently nor impatiently—just waited, very still, and looked at him, and let him see the antipathy in her eyes. Inside, she wanted to scream, to hit him, to hurt him—but that was inside. She knew her face showed only what she wanted it to.

He came nearer to her, tall, powerful, an animal who could change from calmness to passion in moments.

But never again—not with her. He must not touch
her. She moved slightly away, and saw his eyes narrow
imperceptibly. 'Your car,' he said. 'Have you heard?'

'What?' The words didn't register.

'Has the garage phoned you yet about your car?'

'Oh. Not yet. But they will, later.' Why don't you
go away? she added silently, inwardly.

And he did. He walked away from her, going towards the door, stooping to stroke Fiona as he did so.
Then he turned and looked back at her, briefly, almost
as if without thought. But she saw, for a second, something in his eyes which frightened her, and she turned
away and switched on the vacuum cleaner again as if
it would erase the memory of that glance. It had been
only a moment, but it was as if it had lasted for ever,
timeless. It was as if it said—wait, oh, just you wait.

She put her hand to her burning forehead when he
had gone, and she felt faint and dizzy.

And somewhere, a few more threads were drawn
into place, and things moved inexorably onwards, into
a strange and complicated design.


It happened that evening when Emma returned from
the hospital thirty miles away. Kim was drinking coffee
in the kitchen. She was alone, Mrs Barnes having gone
out with her husband after the washing up was all
done, to visit some relatives in the village several miles
away. Kim had her feet up on a stool and was sipping
the hot sweet coffee, tired after a full and busy day—
when Emma walked in, flung her handbag down on the
table, and burst into tears.

Tiredness forgotten, Kim was instantly on her feet,

arms going out to comfort the older woman. 'Emma love, what is it?'

'It's Bill——' Emma sobbed.

'He's not——' Kim's heart contracted painfully.

'No. He's not worse—but they want him to have an operation in a couple of days—some new thing—and it could mean all the difference——'

'Here, sit down, the water's hot, I'll make you coffee and you can tell me all about it——' the worst fears were dispelled, and Kim was in control. She made Emma sit down, pushed the stool before her, put her legs on it, and went to make a cup of coffee at the stove.

'Now, tell me all.' She handed Emma the brimming beaker. 'Drink first.'

Emma smiled weakly. 'Thanks. It's all right, I'm feeling better already. I was just so mixed up——' she took a long swallow. 'It's just—I want to be there—be by his side, before and after—and it's impossible.' She sighed.

Kim was filled with a sudden quiet strength. 'Why?' she demanded. 'Why is it impossible?'

'Because, cuckoo, I have a hotel to run.'

'Correction. Mr and Mrs Barnes and *I* have a hotel to run.'

'But——' Emma looked up, and the dawning wonder on her face was beautiful to see. It told Kim all she needed to know. She knelt by her cousin's side.

'You're the cuckoo, not me. Don't you see? Your place is by your husband's side. Heavens, that might be why I'm here—there are only three—well, four— guests, and Mrs Barnes is a super cook—and I can clean and tidy and dust and say yes ma'am, no ma'am with the best of them—and I bet if I asked the Colonel he'd wash up——'

A stifled giggle escaped Emma and Kim hugged her. 'You make it sound so easy, Kim—but you came to help, not to run——'

'Ssh! That's enough. The decision's not really yours to make, is it? I've already made up my mind, and I'll bet the Barnes' will say——'

'Oh, Kim, do you really mean it? Could I——'

'Yes.' Kim stood up. 'You could—you can—you will. You'd better start getting packed. Now, what do they all have for supper? Horlicks and biscuits?'

'Something like that.' Emma smiled, the relief on her face shining though. 'Bill sends you his love, by the way. He'll want to give you a big hug when I tell him what you've just said.'

'That's good enough for me,' said Kim. 'Now, get to bed. I'll stay up till Mr and Mrs Barnes get in, and tell them. You get a good night's sleep and in the morning you'll know you're doing the right thing.'

'I think I know it now,' agreed Emma quietly. 'I don't deserve a cousin like you.'

'Listen, Emma, you were wonderful to me, you and Bill, when Mother died. I haven't forgotten that. If you like, we'll say I'm returning the favour. Go on—off you go to bed, you look tired out. Will you be able to stay at the hospital?'

Emma nodded. 'Yes. They suggested it. I can do so much for him, you see. But I told them I couldn't——'

'Then I suggest you phone them on your way up, and tell them you can.' She handed Emma the beaker. 'Or shall I?'

'No, I'll do it now. Goodnight, Kim—and thanks.'

Kim watched her go. She waited a few minutes, quietly looking round the kitchen, then she went out towards the lounge to ask the guests—her guests—what they would like for their supper.

The two sisters and the Colonel were watching television, but of Luke there was no sign. Kim had not considered the implications of her decision to help Emma, but she did so as she returned kitchenwards. She would, unavoidably, have more contact with Luke. Not that it made any difference—Emma's happiness was far more important than anything else.

It wasn't until much later, when she went to her room after talking to Mr and Mrs Barnes, and finding that they were only too willing to help, that she discovered the reason for Luke's absence, and in part, an answer to her unspoken question.

She heard quite clearly from his room below the unmistakable rat-a-tat of a typewriter being used at speed. He was still writing. And she wondered, briefly, but didn't really care, whether he was successful at it.

The next morning she found out.

Emma had been seen safely off, with fond farewells all round, the two sisters—Kim had privately nick-named Miss Dines 'the Dragon'—had gone out clad in stout walking shoes and capes, the Colonel had re-tired to the plant-filled conservatory to continue his memoirs, and the Barnes' were out shopping. Kim was in charge of the hotel. The downstairs rooms had been well vacuumed and dusted, Fiona slept—illegally—on one of the settees in the lounge, and Kim went up to the first floor to continue the seemingly never-ending task of vacuuming. It's like the Forth bridge, she thought. No sooner finished one end than you have to start again at the other—and the delicious thought of actually vacuuming the Forth Bridge made her laugh.

Until she reached Luke's room, gave a perfunctory knock, then went in. She had seen him go out immediately after breakfast. What she hadn't seen was that he had returned. He was sitting at a table by the window, typewriter in front of him, sheets of typescript scattered all over the desk. And the reason she had heard no sound was because he was writing something on one of the sheets in pencil. He turned, looked, and then stood up. His face was very hard.

'I'm sorry,' she began. 'I thought you were out.'

'And as you see, I'm not.' He was waiting for her to go.

'I'll do your room later.' She started to back out.

'Wait.' He ran his fingers through his hair. 'You'd better do it now, I'll be here all day.'

Kim felt a constriction in her throat. 'It doesn't matter——'

'Yes, it does, damn it! Do you think I want interrupting every five minutes?' Quick temper flared, she saw a muscle move in his dark jaw, and with great self-control she resisted the temptation to tell him to go to hell.

'Very well. I'll only be two minutes.' She switched on the vacuum cleaner and it buzzed into life. Luke had made his bed, and apart from the incredibly untidy desk, everything else was neat. He stood by his desk and watched her silently, his whole demeanour one of seething impatience. And Kim, perversely, took her time, did every inch of the carpet thoroughly, and then took the duster out of her apron pocket.

'Leave that,' he said.

'But I——'

'I don't care if the dust is a foot thick. I can live with it.'

There were so many things she was tempted to say. Only one thing stopped her. He was a paying guest, and she was, albeit temporarily, working for him. She swallowed down all retorts. 'Very well. I'm sorry to have disturbed you.'

'Are you?' The hard eyes mocked her. He partly turned away, as if dismissing her. It was the very arrogance of his stance that caused her to retort:

'You can be as rude as you like, *Mr* Savage, if that pleases you—and I won't answer back. You're a guest here, and I'm acting proprietress, so if it gives you satisfaction to be impolite, go ahead. Perhaps you'll be good enough, later on today, to let me know if it's convenient for me to come in at some time tomorrow.' And she opened the door and began to push the vacuum cleaner out.

'Wait. What do you mean?'

She paused by the door. 'My cousin has gone to stay at the hospital with her sick husband, and I've taken her place. So you can be as boorish as you want —for as long as you're here.' She went out, closing the door very softly behind her.

Then, later, something very strange happened. It was after lunch, at which only Colonel Pickering and Luke had eaten, the sisters having taken sandwiches out with them. Everyone was quiet, and Kim was passing through the hall on her way to the kitchen when the phone rang at the reception counter. She picked it up. 'Rykin Hotel, good afternoon.'

A foreign voice spoke, a man's, the voice deep. 'You have a Mr Nicholas Severn there, please?'

'Mr Nicholas Severn? Just one moment.' She knew there wasn't, but there might be something on the advance booking chart which lay on the desk before her. She had not seen the man come out of the lounge, and until Luke picked up the telephone and spoke, she had not heard him either.

'I'm sorry—there's no one of that name here,' he said, and put the telephone back on its rest. Even in the midst of her sheer astonishment at his outrageous action, Kim was aware of one thing. *He had spoken in a very pronounced Scottish accent!*

'What!' She whirled round. 'How *dare* you!' She was blazing, all good resolutions at being the perfect substitute for Emma forgotten in her stupefaction. She still didn't believe it—but it had happened. 'How *dare* you do such a thing! You have no *right* to touch that——'

Luke stood looking at her, and even in her own astonishment she could see that he was as angry as she. That only made it even more puzzling, especially when he spoke. 'But I did,' he said. 'And you couldn't even begin to guess why, could you?'

'No. That was someone asking after a guest, and you had no——'

'He was asking after me.'

'You! Don't be so damned stupid! He was asking about a Nicholas Severn——'

'Yes. My pen name.' Luke stood there, and for a moment he was all powerful, awesome, a remote stranger whom she might never have seen before....

'You're mad!' she gasped.

'I'm not. I'll even tell you who that was. Ever heard of Ivan Zolto, the film producer?'

'Yes, but what has that to do with you?' She was bemused, dazed, wondering if she had strayed out of normality into some bizarre film herself.

'He's trying to find me—and I don't want him to.'

She stared at him. 'You'll be telling me next you're a film star——'

'No. A writer.'

'Nicholas Severn?' Light dawned. Slowly. '*You're*——'

'Yes.'

'But you——'

'But I what? I'm Luke Savage? Yes, I know that, thanks. I don't write under my own name. Nicholas is my second christian name, and Severn was my mother's—but you wouldn't have remembered *that* from three years ago, would you?' The cutting tones lashed her with a cruel force, making her gasp. 'There were other things to do, weren't there?'

'I don't think we need——' she began faintly, her head throbbing in sudden pain.

'Yes, we do. Oh yes, we do, Kim Sheridan, *Miss* Kim Sheridan, of the sweet voice and the feminine ways—oh yes——'

Anguished, unable to bear any more of the inexorable voice that pounded in her mind, Kim struck him hard across the face, hearing, as if from a distance, the resounding slap that echoed and re-echoed in the small hall—and Luke, his face suddenly that of a man in torment, caught hold of her and crushed her to him. 'You will listen to me,' he breathed. 'You will!'

'Let me *go*!' She struggled violently, arching her body away from that relentless hold. In vain—until suddenly she was free, and he had turned away, was leaning on the desk, white-faced, as if he realised too late what he had done. Kim fled, back to the safety of the kitchen where she slammed the door behind her and stood with her back against it, knuckles pressed to her mouth. Luke's violence—and her own—had frightened her. In a few moments, everything had erupted, like a sudden storm. Then, shakily, she went over to the table and sat down.

It was there, a minute later, that Luke found her. He came into the room without knocking and closed the door behind him. Kim jumped to her feet, eyes desperately searching the room for a weapon—anything—to defend herself.

'I'm not going to touch you,' he said harshly.

She swallowed. 'Then stay where you are.' They were alone, or virtually so. Colonel Pickering, safely ensconced in his conservatory, writing busily, was too far away to hear her shout—and he was slightly deaf anyway, and both Mr and Mrs Barnes were gardening.

'All right, I will. I want to say——'

'Don't bother to apologise,' she cut in swiftly.

'I wasn't going to,' was the surprising answer. 'I was going to tell you that if anyone rings for Nicholas Severn again I want you to tell them you've never heard of him.'

'And why should I?' she retorted.

'Because I'm a guest—and you're working here, as you reminded me this morning.'

'*That* was before your outrageous behaviour. As far as I'm concerned you can leave as soon as you like.'

'I have no intention of doing so—until *I* choose to go. Do I make myself clear?' The arrogance was there all right, he wasn't even bothering to hide it. He stood there, straight and tall, facing her, and his eyes were cold and hard, and his anger was a potent wave of force reaching across the room, touching her, surrounding her. . . .

'You make yourself quite clear. And as you're so obviously frightened of anyone knowing you're here, I'll say I've never heard of Nicholas Severn——'

'I'm not frightened,' he cut in. 'Merely working.'

'I don't want to know what you're doing,' she said breathlessly, 'it's no concern of mine——'

'Too right it isn't!'

She looked away from him, breaking herself free of the spell. 'If you've said all you came to, I'd appreciate it if you'd leave this kitchen.'

There was a moment's silence, then: 'Very well, I will.'

He turned as if to go out. 'Just a moment,' Kim said. 'What if anyone phones asking for you by your real name?'

'No one should. I told no one.'

'But somebody obviously has an idea——'

'A try, that's all.' He paused, looking her up and down in a way that made her go warm. Hastily, nervous, she said:

'And why did you put on that ridiculous Scottish accent when you picked up the phone?'

A ghost of a smile flickered across his face. 'Why? So that he wouldn't recognise my voice, that's all.'

She lifted her chin. 'So you must be scared.'

'God! Are you stupid? They're after me for a *book*, woman, not my life. Nobody has ever frightened me, not even you——' the last three words very soft, almost menacing. 'But I want peace and quiet. Or is that too difficult for you to understand?'

'I wouldn't say that's what you're getting at the moment, then,' she retorted with spirit. Those three words had stung more than she cared to admit. 'Seeing that you seem to be spending most of your time arguing——'

'With *you*?' Soft, in a way that sent trickles down

her spine. 'You I can cope with. I told you—you're nothing.'

'Get out!'

'I'm going. I've better things to do than waste my time talking to someone as two-faced as——' Breathless, in a rush, she launched herself at him, motives unclear even to herself—yet she didn't want to hear any more, and she wasn't going to, even if it meant pushing him out of the kitchen forcibly. Which idea, she realised a moment later, was about as possible as shifting the Rock of Gibraltar by hand.

Luke caught hold of her arm and whirled her away from him. Incensed, she landed out with her free arm —and that too was then caught and held so that she was as helpless as a fly in a web.

'You little bitch!' his voice shook. The red mark faded on his cheek, and his eyes had gone very dark and shadowed. 'My God, I'd like to——' he stopped.

'Beat me? I'd just bet you would!' Kim breathed. She was trembling with fear—and with his touch, which burned like fire, and the whole room quivered with the startling tension, so that her body went weak.

'It's what you deserve,' he retorted harshly. 'But I wouldn't lower myself.'

'You couldn't get any lower, you—you beast!' she exclaimed. She twisted feverishly to escape, but his strength was such that it had no effect. Then suddenly he pulled her towards him, took hold of her hair so that she couldn't move her head an inch, and kissed her with a savage intensity. Contemptuous, she felt the pressure of his lips burning hers like fire—then he released her and towered over her.

'I just wanted to remember what it was like,' he said, 'and now I do. Don't worry, I won't touch you again—that was enough to last me a lifetime,' and he wiped his hand across his mouth as if to erase the memory.

Shattered, wretchedly and utterly humiliated, Kim turned away, to lean over the table. She had no breath left to answer him, and the tears in her eyes blinded her. Then the door slammed shut, and she was alone. Shakily she sat down, and the memories she had tried so hard to forget came rushing back. She put her face in her hands and sat very still as she saw again Luke's face as it had been three years ago, when he had found her in the arms of his best friend. He hadn't given her a chance to explain the truth. Perhaps that had hurt her more than anything else—the knowledge that he chose to believe Paul's word of what had happened. Kim stroked a pattern on the table, not seeing what she was doing, recalling only the violence of his words as he had faced her, there in that living room in Paul's flat, while Paul crawled to his feet again after Luke's knock-out blow. 'So it is true,' he had said, and his face had been whiter than she had ever seen it before. 'You've been having an affair with him behind my back —and all the time I trusted you—I *trusted* you absolutely.'

'But I only came because——' she had begun, desperately sick at what she saw in his eyes—and then Paul had spoken. Blood trickling from his cut lip, standing supported by the mantelpiece, Paul had spat out: 'I told you, Luke, but you wouldn't believe me.

Now—get out!' And Luke had gone, and she had never seen him after that—until yesterday. She had looked at Paul after Luke's violent exit. 'Why—why?' she had whispered.

His reply had been shattering, and yet, in a way, something she had known all along. 'If I can't have you,' he had said, dabbing at his bruised mouth, 'I'm damned sure he's not going to.'

'You—you know you mean nothing to me.'

'But he doesn't——' a twisted grin. 'Who do you think made sure he'd arrive at the right moment? I listened out, I waited, I kissed you at the right time, didn't I?'

'You're mad!' she had gasped. 'I'm going to tell him——'

'It's too late. He won't listen to you. I told him we were lovers.'

'What?' Her whole world had collapsed at that moment.

'I told him we had been for a long time. Do you think I'd have introduced you two if I'd known you were going to marry him? Kim, just give me another chance——'

'I never want to see you again!' And she had rushed out. She never had—or Luke—because a week later her mother had died, and that blow was even more shattering. Emma had been the salvation of her. Kim looked up at the window. She had learned her lesson —never trust a man. That Luke could have believed.... But there was more, that she didn't know about. She was soon to find out what it was.

# CHAPTER THREE

EMMA telephoned that evening, and Kim knew she had done the right thing in telling her to go. It helped a little to alleviate her misery at the afternoon's events, which still had the power to disturb her by the memory, although she had tried desperately to put Luke's actions out of her mind. It was strange, the difference in his behaviour when they met with others present. She had served dinner with Mrs Barnes, and she knew that nobody in that dining room was aware of anything amiss—and later, when she had gone into the lounge, and he had been watching television with Miss Dines and Mrs Beaumont, he had helped her move a coffee table in readiness for their supper. Miss Dines was behaving very archly, her voice teasing as she made some comment on his gallantry. Under normal circumstances Kim would have found it amusing—but the circumstances were far from normal, and could never be while he was around. The trilling voice followed her as she left the room: 'Sit over *here*, Mr Savage, I'm sure you'll find it far more comfortable than that chair——'

Kim closed the door. Oh God, she thought. If only that woman knew the half of it! But she never would. She went out to the kitchen, repeating to herself: 'One cocoa, one Horlicks, one coffee'—and tea for Colonel

Pickering who had decided, on some whim, to stay in the conservatory because, as he had told Kim earlier, chapter thirty-three of his memoirs was working out very nicely indeed—she wondered if Luke had mentioned that he was a writer. And she knew the answer already. He had come for peace and quiet, and to write. She was probably the only person in the hotel to know —and that she had discovered only by chance. She had heard of the name Nicholas Severn, but never in her wildest imaginings had she visualised Luke as being the same man. His first book, published only months previously. Perhaps, she caught her breath in her throat—perhaps it had been the one he had been struggling with when they had been together. What strange tricks fate played sometimes! It had already been made into a film, a spy thriller, set in Finland; the title? She frowned. What was it? *The Tangled Web*—that was it.

She went into the kichen and put on the kettle, filled a pan with milk and put it on the stove to warm. Mrs Barnes bustled in from the pantry wiping her hands on her apron. 'The usual?'

'Yes. Tea, coffee, cocoa, Horlicks—why, oh, why don't they all have the same thing?'

Mrs Barnes chuckled. 'Because they're guests, that's why. You be thankful there's only four of them. We had someone once who insisted on Russian tea last thing at night—ugh!' She pulled a face. 'Imagine slicing up lemons at eleven o'clock of an evening!'

Kim laughed, putting Luke out of her mind. 'If I make the drinks, will you take them in? The Colonel's

in the conservatory. I want an early night, then I'll do
breakfast in the morning.'

'Are you sure?' The housekeeper looked concerned.
'Albert and I can manage, you know—and you're not
really here to——'

'Yes, I am. It was me told Emma to go, don't you
worry. I'll be up at six, so you can have a lie-in till
eight.'

'Ah, seven's more like it, love. Couldn't stay in bed
if I tried. I'm one of your early birds, you know.'

'Then,' said Kim, 'you shall have a cup of tea in bed
at seven. How does that suit you?'

'Lovely.' Mrs Barnes sighed. 'You'll spoil us.'

'Good. Emma sends her love, by the way. I'm off
now.' Kim had been busily mixing the drinks, the
kettle had boiled, the milk was snatched from disaster
with seconds to spare, the tray was ready. Kim absent-
mindedly picked up a biscuit from the plate on the tray
and bit into it. 'See you at seven. Goodnight.'

'G'night, Kim dear. Sleep well.'

'I will.' She yawned. 'I'm exhausted!'

Within five minutes of putting her head down on the
pillow, Kim was sound asleep. Everything was working out nicely to plan, was the last thought in her mind
before sleep claimed her. Everything....

In the cold grey light of pre-dawn, when the birds were
still debating about waking up, Kim washed and
dressed, then went down to the darkened kitchen and
roused Fiona from her slumbers in her basket at the
corner by the fireplace.

'Come on, old girl, outside,' she whispered, and opened the back door, letting a blast of icy air in. Fiona padded reluctantly out, and Kim's day began. She filled the kettle, then lit the fire, put out the breakfast plates and went into the dining room to check that the places were set. Everyone slept, all was silent and shadowy.

By the time she had drunk her cup of tea, the first rays of the sun were reaching in through the windows, and although there was a faint ground mist, it promised to be a warm day. Fiona sat on the rug, scratching herself, and Kim hummed a tune as she sat in the rocking chair in front of the crackling log fire. Her day was planned. Before she took the Barnes' tea up at seven there were the dining room windows to clean. She had noticed them the previous day. That was job number one. After that, breakfast, then vacuuming, then. . . . Mentally Kim went over her list, ticking them off on her fingers. Running a hotel, she decided several minutes later, as she wiped vigorously at the dining room windows, perched on a chair, was a piece of cake really. Hard work, yes, but predictable. And as long as you were organised mentally, everything fell into place. She hummed a tune, and the windows began to shine, and she realised with faint surprise that she quite enjoyed cleaning windows. She squinted at a corner she had missed, gave it a final wipe, picked up the bucket of water, replaced the chair, and went out to the kitchen.

It was only when she went up with the two cups of

tea to Mr and Mrs Barnes that the day started to go disastrously wrong.

She knocked and waited, then knocked again, more loudly. Silence. 'Mrs Barnes,' whispered Kim, then, after a few moments, 'Mrs Barnes, are you awake?'

There was a muffled groan, then the sound of something being knocked over. A prickle of fear touched Kim's neck. She rattled the door handle, pushed, but the door was locked. Then, faintly, so faintly that she scarcely heard, came the whisper: 'Kim——'

'Can you open the door?' She had put the tea-tray down on the floor, and knelt to the keyhole, but could see nothing. Silence.

'Mrs Barnes, knock if you can hear me.' She pressed her ear to the door and heard an almost imperceptible rapping sound.

'Are you ill? Knock once if you are.' There was one sharp knock, then silence. The fear had gone. Kim's mind, trained to deal with minor emergencies in school, became very clear, razor-sharp.

'Don't try and answer. I'm going to get help. I'll be back as soon as I can.' She went quickly away. There was only one person she could ask, and nothing else mattered at the moment save the fact that someone needed help.

She knocked at Luke's door as loudly as she dared, then waited in a fever of impatience. She heard nothing for a few moments, then his voice, half asleep, 'Who is it?'

'It's me, Kim—please can you come——'

'What the hell——' The door was flung open and

he stood there, hair tousled, face grim—a dressing gown dragged on, it seemed. 'What the bloody hell——'

'It's the housekeeper and her husband.' She cut him off neatly in mid-swear, knowing there had been more to come, and not caring. 'They're ill, and I can't get in their room——'

He was wide awake, instantly wide awake. He looked down at her. 'Where's their room?'

'Upstairs. Number fifteen.'

'Give me five seconds to get some trousers on. The door's locked, you say? Go and get the master keys, then take them up.' He closed the door and she fled down the stairs. She should have thought of that herself—why on earth hadn't she? She grabbed the ring of keys from their hook behind the desk and ran up again, up the two flights to see Luke waiting, listening, outside their door.

He took them from her, found the one marked fifteen, and opened the door. He took one look inside and turned to Kim. 'Go and phone for a doctor.' He didn't waste time. As she ran down she heard his voice faintly from above: 'Kim's gone to phone—just lie still——' The voice faded. She didn't even know what she had to say on the telephone, but that didn't matter. In a way she couldn't define, she knew he had taken over, and somehow she became calmer.

She found the number, picked up the telephone, and began to dial.

The delayed shock came later when, as she prepared

breakfast in the kitchen, Kim dropped a plate because her hand had simply refused to work. She sat down and counted to ten very slowly, then held up her fingers. They shook with a fine tremor. Very deliberately she calmed herself, took a few deep breaths, and stood up. There's no point in you going to pieces, she told herself severely. You're on your own now, go get cracking. Fiona watched her anxiously from her seat by the fire. 'It's up to us,' Kim said. The prospect was, to say the least, daunting. Why, oh, why had the Barnes' eaten that prawn cocktail at the friends' they had popped out to visit the previous evening? They had only been gone an hour, after dinner, that had been all, but the damage was done. Both had come down during the night with a severe attack of food poisoning —as had, the doctor informed them, five other people in the village. He had whisked them off with him in his Land Rover to the local cottage hospital.

Now, two hours later, Kim was on her own. She had heard movements and voices as the two sisters rose, then Colonel Pickering's boom, and she swallowed. This was it. The bacon sizzled gently under the grill together with the sausages and tomatoes, and the five eggs poached in the pan. All she had to do was take everything in.

The kitchen door opened and Luke stood there. 'The doctor gave me a few phone numbers of people he thought might come in and help,' he said. His voice was quite impersonal. 'I tried them, but it's no go. Staff are impossible to find at this time of the year up here.'

'I know.' She moved the pan of eggs slightly from the heat. 'I didn't imagine otherwise.' She lifted her chin. 'I'll manage.'

'You won't.'

'I don't have much choice,' she answered. 'The breakfast is ready—if you'll excuse me?' She began to count the plates she had set out.

'Have you eaten?'

'No. But I will—after.' Why didn't he go *away*?

He shook his head. 'You can't manage alone, you must know that. Are there any more guests expected today?'

'No—I checked. A couple arrive next week, but until then there's only the four of you. Please—the breakfast is ready—I must——'

'Can you get your cousin back?'

'No! She mustn't know about this. Her place is with her husband.'

'Then that settles it.' He walked over from the door. 'Okay, get the trolley ready. Three breakfasts—I'll take them in.'

'Three? But——'

'I'll have mine out here. This is where the staff eat, isn't it?'

'Your sense of humour is bizarre to say the least,' she said, her lip trembling. 'I don't find you at all funny.'

'I'm not trying to be, I'm deadly serious. You need help. Okay, you've got it.' He moved past her to the giant cooker and picked up the tongs. 'How many rashers each? Two or three?'

'Three, and a sausage, but——' She was bewildered, utterly and absolutely bewildered.

'You'd better get the toaster going, hadn't you?'

The hot food was being transferred to the plates as he spoke, and he looked at her, a hard level glance. 'Go on, do it.'

Kim took a deep breath. 'You—*you're* going to help?'

'Yes. Do you find it very strange? It isn't. I'll explain later—after I've told our guests all about it. Right,' he stared at the plates, 'hmm, that's it. I'll be back in a minute. Keep those eggs warm—and get the toast started.' Then he was gone. Kim, feeling a sense of detachment, began to feed the toaster with slices of white bread.

Fifteen minutes later she was sitting eating her breakfast at the kitchen table with Luke. She looked up from her plate. 'Why?' she said simply. 'Why?'

He shrugged. 'I wouldn't see anyone lumbered like you've been. If you'd worked here for years—fine, you'd cope. But you haven't. I can cook, and I can wield a nifty duster if I have to.' He speared a rasher of bacon. 'I came here to write—the details of that I will not bore you with—but the book is set in a hotel —in this one, as a matter of fact. I like to get the feel of a place while I'm actually writing about it, and I came here years ago, so it won't hurt for me to go into it in greater depth. And another reason is, it'll get Miss Dines and the Colonel off my back. The Colonel is okay, but when you've heard about his campaigns in the Libyan desert twice, believe me, that's enough.

As for Miss Dines——' he paused, 'she's a human leech. I need her like I need a hole in the head. So, I eat out here—she thinks I'm extremely noble—I'm not, but at least she'll never know.' He looked at her. 'My reasons are extremely selfish.'

Kim met his eyes, and there was nothing there of what had once been between them. He spoke like a cool stranger, his voice impersonal, and that was the best way. And all that he said made sense. And she did need help, oh, how she needed it!

'Then—thank you,' she said quietly. 'I can't say any more. I'm still rather numb——'

'Then don't. I'm not asking for medals,' he answered, and his voice had gone harsher. 'And as far as anything else is concerned, we're strangers.'

'Yes.' It was the only way. It had to be so. 'But your writing——'

'I'll find time for that. I'll write in the evenings instead. The Barnes' should be okay in a few days, by which time I'll be able to write with authority about hotel management.' He stood up and took his empty plate to the sink. 'Coffee?'

'I'll make it.'

'Finish what you're eating. I'll do it. The dog—when does she get fed?'

'Oh, in the evening.'

'You must make a list of all the food we need for the next few days. Is there a freezer?'

'Yes. It's full.'

'I'll check it after.' He handed her a cup full of coffee. 'I helped out in a restaurant, in the dim and distant past, when I was a student—you don't need to worry, I know how to boil potatoes, and I'm a dab hand with roast chicken.'

'I'm not worried,' Kim said quietly. She looked up at him. 'After all that's already happened, I'm past that stage. We'll manage somehow.'

'Yes, we will. And I'll bet they——' Luke jerked his head towards the dining room, 'won't even notice the difference.'

'Let's see that they don't.' She drank some of the coffee. He had made it very strong; perhaps for a reason.

The telephone suddenly shrilled, and she picked up the extension. 'Good morning, Rykin Hotel.' Please, not someone wanting a room, she prayed silently.

'Can I speak to Mr Savage?' It was a woman's voice, pitched low—and very confidently. Kim had one second to think, and pointed at Luke, eyes warning. He shook his head, walked over quietly to her and made a negative gesture with his hand.

'I'm sorry,' she answered. The delay had been fractional. 'But we don't have anyone of that name here.'

'Are you sure? Who are you?'

There was something in that quietly confident voice that prickled at Kim's sensitivity.

'I'm the acting proprietress,' she answered, in the most beautifully modulated voice, 'and yes, I'm *quite* sure. Have you tried any other hotels in the locality? I can give you a few names——'

'That won't be necessary.' The voice had become sharper. 'Look, he could be staying there under another name—if I describe him——'

'I'm also quite sure, madam,' Kim cut in smoothly, 'that none of our guests would do that.' She injected a faint note of shocked concern into her voice, and saw the brief grin touch Luke's face. He could hear every word, that was obvious.

'He's about six foot three, dark-haired—good-looking in a gipsy sort of way—wears *very* casual clothes——' There was a pause, as if the woman on the other end waited for Kim's affirmation. And Kim, prompted by some imp of mischief she didn't fully understand, said:

'Oh, wait. There's a Colonel Pickering. About fifty-five—tall—oh dear, though, he's going bald—would that be——'

There was a sharp click, and then the dialling tone. Kim replaced the receiver thoughtfully. That had been an angry click, if ever she had heard one!

Luke shook his head. 'I think,' he said slowly, 'you'd better let me answer it next time it rings.'

'Be my guest,' she answered. 'I rather think she was annoyed.'

'Yes.' He turned away. Clearly he had no intention of telling Kim who the caller had been. And she didn't want to know. She went over to the table to finish her coffee. What next? she wondered. Could there be much more? A few hours later, she found out that there could.

Kim saw the maroon Rolls-Royce from the window of the bedroom that afternoon. She watched in fascina-

tion as it glided silently up the drive, then stopped on
the gravel outside the front entrance. Quick as a flash
she was out of the room and running downstairs—
and nearly collided with Luke, on his way up. He
grabbed her to stop her falling. 'What the——'

'A car—a *Rolls*—you should see it!' she gasped.

'Oh God, *no*—what colour?'

The question threw her. 'Purple—no, maroon.'

A brief, unprintable epithet followed. Then he
looked, as if measuring the distance from where he
stood to his room. 'Look—sorry, Kim—just get rid of
him, will you? Do anything, say anything you like, but
you don't know me, you haven't seen me——'

'But your car,' she interrupted, as they heard the
outer door crash open, and Fiona begin to bark in welcome, 'it's at the front——'

'Hell and damnation!'

'Look, I'll try. Who——' she lowered her voice to a
whisper. They were out of sight of the entrance hall,
but only just—'Who *is* it?'

'Him,' he mouthed. 'Ivan Zolto. And he doesn't
usually take no for an answer.'

'Thanks!' There was no time for more. Composing
herself, putting a bright smile on her face, Kim walked
slowly down the stairs, and saw the huge man who
paced the hall, ignoring Fiona completely. He looked
up at her.

'Ah,' he said. 'At last! Someone comes!' It was un-
mistakably the same voice, the same fractured English
that she had heard on the telephone.

'I'm sorry, sir,' she said very sweetly. 'Were you

waiting? Can I help you?'

'I hope so.' His boom was worse than the Colonel's. She would have sworn that the grandfather clock vibrated in the corner. 'I am looking for someone—one of your guests.'

'Oh!' She sounded very pleased. 'May I have her name?'

'*His* name. Nick Severn—or you may know him as Luke Savage.' He was completely bald, hugely built, and wore a thick tartan suit that could better have been viewed through sunglasses. Kim had never actually seen orange of that shade on tartan before.

'Oh dear,' she looked crestfallen. 'I'm awfully sorry——'

He began to laugh. It started as a chuckle and became a roar of sound that filled the hotel and probably shook the rafters. 'What has he told you, hey? To say that he is not here?'

'I'm afraid I don't understand, sir.' She managed to sound prim, but with difficulty. There was something quite irresistible about the man. Larger than life, his personality enveloped her in a kind of warm conspiracy. He didn't take no for an answer—she could well believe that. But there seemed something quite apart from ruthlessness about him. He had a certain gigantic charm.

'My dear girl,' he shook his head, rosy cheeks beaming, 'you don't fool me for a moment. His car is outside——' he smote his forehead with a ham-like hand. 'Such a car! I have seen better on scrap heaps—but it is his. Now, where is he?'

'I'm here, Ivan,' came Luke's voice, and he walked down the stairs.

'My dear boy!' Luke was clasped in a bearlike hug, and Ivan Zolto turned to her. 'You see? I knew. Why are you hiding away up here, eh? Tell me that?'

'I'm working.'

'So? You are working? Good—good—but why the secrecy? You know we have business to talk about, like this book you are writing. I want to see it—okay, so you have told me what it is about and where it is set, and I am coming up to see for myself this beautiful Lake District you talk so much about——'

'Look, why don't we have a coffee and we can talk?'

'Coffee? *Coffee?* Who is drinking coffee?' He produced a flask from a pocket of the startling jacket. 'Vodka, my dear fellow. Two glasses, please, miss——'

'I'd better introduce you,' cut in Luke. 'Kim, this is Ivan Zolto who is world-famous, as you well know—Ivan, this is Kim Sheridan, with whom I'm at present running the hotel.'

'Running the hotel? You joke, my dear boy.' Ivan turned to Kim with a shrug of his huge shoulders. 'What is this running the hotel—he is writing a book for me—yes?'

'Well, yes,' admitted Kim. 'But——'

'Kim, I think you'd better get two glasses if you will, while I explain to Ivan what's going on. We'll be in the lounge.' Luke put his arm round the older man's shoulder and drew him away. Kim could hear his voice, soothing, quiet—but firm: 'You see, Ivan, three people have suddenly been taken ill, and Kim was left alone——' the voice faded. Kim, feeling, quite faintly, that she was in the middle of some exotic dream, floated kitchenwards for the glasses. It would all come out right, in a hundred years or so. There was absolutely no point in bothering or worrying about anything. She no longer wondered what might happen next. Because she was quite sure that something startling would, and she was becoming immune to shocks. At least she hoped so.

The words that greeted her when she reached the lounge were startling. 'This is marvellous! To step in and take over like that—I like that.' Ivan Zolto looked up and surveyed her with bright yellowy gold eyes. 'And I will be no trouble at all.'

She looked at Luke in desperation. Had she heard correctly? Did he mean what she thought he did?

She saw the answer in Luke's eyes before he spoke. He did.

'But, Ivan, you're used to the best of everything—we're but two struggling beginners—no *haute cuisine*——'

'Ah! The simple life! Yes, what a change. It appeals to my sense of humour. It will be like the old days—and we can talk about your book——'

Just for a second, Kim glimpsed what was in Luke's eyes—and she began to laugh. Helplessly, for no reason at all, the funny side of it struck her so strongly that she couldn't stop. She sat down in one of the chairs, doubled up, powerless to escape the laughter that bubbled up inside her. Then Ivan joined in.

Wiping her eyes, she gasped: 'I'm sorry——'

'Sorry?' Ivan roared. 'You are delightful. Quite delightful.' He lumbered to his feet. 'One moment, there is something in my car——' and he vanished, still shaking. Luke glanced at Kim.

'Thanks,' he said drily. 'Thanks a million.'

Kim sobered. 'I—I couldn't help it. I'm sorry.'

His eyes were hard. 'No, I don't think you could. But you've just lumbered us, unless I'm very mistaken, with one extra guest—and maybe more. Where Ivan is, others are not far behind. He may be alone now, but you can be damn sure that not a dozen miles away are a few of his friends, just waiting for word of what he's doing. That man is the biggest extrovert I know.'

'What can we do?' she whispered.

A corner of his mouth twitched. 'Not a lot. Ever tried to stop a runaway steamroller?'

'Oh, Luke,' in her anguish she was not aware of the way she spoke his name, 'I feel awful!'

'I don't feel too good myself. He's fine—in small doses—but how much writing do you think I'll manage to do while he's here?'

She bit her lip. 'Can't we tell him we've no room?'

'We can try. Trouble is, he'd look for himself if he felt like it, and see.' He sighed. 'Okay, I can't blame you. It's not your fault he found me, and you did your best to get rid of him tactfully—and he does rather overpower people. We'll manage, somehow.'

Kim looked up, and there were tears in her eyes. Too much had happened in too short a time, and she felt suddenly overwhelmed by it all. She saw Luke's face change, and his expression was one that made her tremble inwardly, that made her heart beat rapidly.

'Don't,' he said.

'It's——' she blinked rapidly. 'I can't help it.'

He closed his eyes, as if in pain. 'I know.' He stood up. 'Stay there, I'll go and talk to him outside for a minute.' As he went past, his hand brushed her shoulder for a second, and she wasn't sure if it was an accident, or deliberate. And she remembered that which she had seen so briefly on his face, and in his eyes. For a moment—just a brief moment—she had seen a man who had once, a long time ago, loved her.

# CHAPTER FOUR

IVAN ZOLTO had gone outside for a bottle of champagne—to celebrate his arrival, he told Kim, as they drank it. The bubbles went up her nose and made her eyes water, but after one glass the world assumed a rosy hue, and it no longer seemed important that he might decide to stay. Because Kim had had an idea—and somehow, some way, she had to get Luke on his own for a minute to tell him about it.

He seemed to have accepted the situation, standing by the fireplace in the lounge, glass in hand, watching them both calmly as Ivan told Kim about all his films, and she listened without managing to get anything more than the occasional yes, oh, I see—how wonderful—in. He needed an audience, that was all.

Then, as the Colonel came in, she seized her chance. She introduced them, saw that Ivan now had a new, even more attentive audience—who knew what was going on in Colonel Pickering's mind? Perhaps he saw the chance for his memoirs to be filmed! It didn't matter. All that was important was the fact that she and Luke could escape.

'We'll have to start dinner, Luke,' she said. 'If you'll excuse us?'

She was waved away by an expansive, beringed hand. 'Yes, yes, of course. You say you actually *met*

Monty, Colonel? That's most interesting. It reminds *me* of the time when *I* was——'

She fled. A few moments later Luke came into the kitchen and Kim turned to him. 'I had an idea,' she said. 'If we can't get rid of him, there's a cottage in the grounds he can stay in. It's not been used for a while, but it's self-contained. He said he'd enjoy the simple life——'

'Do you think he *meant* it?' Luke interrupted dryly.

'I don't know. Does it matter? We can tell him it's that or nothing—especially if, as you say, he'll have a crowd joining him. He can have parties there—he can do what he likes. It's got three bedrooms and lots of space. Come and have a look now.'

He looked doubtfully at the cooker, at the food waiting to be prepared. 'Have we time?'

'*Yes*. If we're quick.'

'Okay.'

It was like being conspirators in some gigantic plot. They ran out of the back door and Kim led him along an overgrown track to the old two-storey stone cottage that stood well hidden from the hotel. Luke whistled his astonishment as he saw it, and Kim pushed the door open.

He looked around him, at the large dusty living room in which they stood, and he nodded his head. 'This place has character,' he said, 'but it needs a lot of cleaning.'

'I can do it in an hour or so,' she answered. 'The main thing is, it's habitable. What do you think?'

'I think you may be right.' He looked at her. 'He

won't leave, I'm certain of that. He wants this book I'm writing.'

'But how can he? You've not even finished it yet, have you?'

'No. But I've told him enough of the plot—you realise what it could mean, don't you?'

Kim glanced at him, bewildered. 'No, I don't.'

'If he buys it to film it—and I'm sure he will—he'll want to film it here. It'll mean a hell of a lot of disruption for your cousins, but it'll also mean a hell of a lot of money for them.'

The words fell into the quiet air, and Kim absorbed them slowly. 'You mean,' she said at last, 'actually *here*, in the hotel?'

'More or less—yes. Mainly the exterior shots. A lot of inside ones can be done in a studio, but yes, that's precisely what I do mean.'

'Oh.' It would mean a world of difference for Emma and Bill. They made a good living from the hotel—but there were problems, as always in any business venture. And if Bill did have to slow down as a result of his operation, it could mean a lot to them. 'I don't know what to say,' she said at last.

'Then don't. I'm just warning you.'

'Yes, I see. It's not up to me anyway, of course——' she paused.

'I know it's not. I'm just trying to let you see what you could be in for. He's a very determined man, and at the moment he's on something of a holiday—as much as anyone like him ever has a holiday—but he'll change our lives for us, whether we like it or not.'

Luke ran his fingers through his hair, and Kim closed her eyes. She wondered if she could cope. He moved towards her. She felt the movement, sensed the nearness, and opened her eyes again.

'I know,' he said quietly. 'I know.'

'What do you know?' She felt strangely breathless; his nearness, whether he knew it or not, was disturbing to her. He still had that power. . . .

'You're—afraid.'

'Yes,' she said softly. But it wasn't entirely for the reasons he thought.

'It's just as well I offered to help. This is partly my fault.' He wasn't attempting to move away. It was as if, just then, they were held in a mutual pact. 'What can I say? I didn't know he'd find me. I thought I'd be safe here, away from everything——' the pause was more significant. It was as if he realised what he had just said. Kim heard his indrawn breath, and said the words she had to say, almost as if under a compulsion.

'And me. You didn't know I'd be here.' It was too late to retract. The words were spoken.

'No, I didn't.' Something seemed to fill the room, echoing silently around them, filling the air—making her senses reel. Then he moved away, as if the stifling atmosphere had affected him as strongly as it had Kim, turned, walked over to the window, and with his back to her, said:

'But you are. I told you before, the past is done.' A moment's hesitation, then: 'We'd better go back and do the dinner. After it, we'll show this place to Ivan— is there enough bedding?'

'Yes. There's a linen room near your bedroom—everything's aired and ready.'

'And if he says yes, then, later tonight, I'll help you clean this place.'

'But you mustn't!' she was horrified. 'You're doing enough—and anyway, there's your writing—and he's come to see *you*!'

'Precisely.' He had turned to face her again. The moment of unutterable tension had passed; everything was as near normal as it ever could be between them. 'It will be a good excuse to keep out of his way. Until his hangers-on arrive, he'll have Miss Dines, her sister, and the Colonel for his audience—and that's all he needs, believe me. As for writing,' he shrugged, 'I'll find time somehow. I need very little sleep. Even he wouldn't be talking at five in the morning. I can write from then until breakfast.' Kim looked at him. She knew every inch of his face. It had never been far from her thoughts in the past three years—but there was something in it now that she had never noticed before; a quiet strength, a determination, and her heart missed a beat. He had been so easy-going—until that awful day in Paul's flat—but there was a side to him she had never seen. She was seeing it now.

'Let's go,' he said, and opened the door. 'One thing —leave the talking to me about this place.'

'Yes, I will.' She went out, and Luke closed the door behind them.

It was difficult to tear Ivan away from his admiring audience after dinner, but they managed it, and when he had seen over the cottage Luke said: 'You know how we're placed, Ivan.' Kim hid a grin, looking away hastily as she did so, pretending to straighten a photograph on the wall. Luke had been carefully paving the way since before dinner, painting a picture of the incredibly hard work Kim was doing on behalf of her cousin until she began to feel like a Cinderella—but with Ivan, it worked. He was so much larger than life himself that the exaggerated phrases Luke used had not seemed out of place at all. Luke was clearly a shrewd psychologist, sensing Ivan's own flair for drama, playing on it, appealing to the man's instinct. 'Kim can't do any more work, and it's impossible to get staff, as I'm sure you can appreciate—but she's so delighted to have you here—as I am too—that this seemed the ideal solution.' Luke waved his arms grandly. 'This would be truly a taste of the simple life for you.'

Kim wouldn't have sworn to it, but there could have been tears in Ivan's eyes. He sighed, very heavily. 'Ah! You are a good friend, Luke. What did I say to Theodora only the other day? Luke is one of the best, I said, and she agreed—you remember Theodora, do you not?'

Luke nodded. 'She'll be coming as well?' Rather faintly, Kim thought.

'Yes, and Zara and Butch—and Clinton, of course.'

Kim couldn't be sure, but Luke seemed to have paled slightly. 'Er—splendid,' he said. 'So you'll be all right for cooks, then?'

'But of course. Theodora is *superb*! She would help
you——'

'No, that won't be necessary,' Luke cut in. 'Thanks
all the same. Right, Ivan, we'll take you back, and then
Kim and I will get cracking—er, will you be phoning
the others?'

'I already did, my dear fellow,' boomed Ivan, 'before dinner. They should be here later this evening.
They're *delighted* that I found you.'

'Yes, I'm sure they are. And I can't wait to meet
them all again. How is Zara? As lovely as ever?'

'Lovelier.' Ivan clasper his hands. 'She grows more
beautiful every day. I am a lucky man, Kim,' his face
was like a child's all of a sudden. 'My fiancée is the
most wonderful woman in the world.' He sighed, shook
his head, then blew his nose on a gigantic red handkerchief. 'Just this morning I left her, and already it seems
like a year. Come, let us go back, in case I am not there
to greet them.' And he led the way out. Kim followed,
and Luke was behind her. She wasn't even sure if she
had imagined it later, but she seemed to hear Luke
utter two faint, despairing words: 'Oh God!'

Half an hour later they left Ivan in the lounge—
talking, of course—and armed with buckets and
brooms, went back to the cottage. And on the way
there Kim discovered that she hadn't imagined Luke's
words after all.

'You'll wonder if you're dreaming when they arrive,'
he said. 'But you won't be. Am I glad you have this
cottage!'

She paused, and took a firmer grip on the carpet

sweeper she carried, which had been in danger of slipping out of her hand. 'Are they awful?' she asked, wide-eyed.

Luke gave a dry laugh. 'Awful? No, I wouldn't say that. Eccentric—way-out—weird perhaps, but not awful.'

They reached the door and she pushed it open. Dust swirled, then settled, and she looked around, sizing up where best to begin. 'What's Theodora like?' she asked him. 'Your voice went rather faint——'

'Did it?' he seemed surprised. 'I thought I'd done rather well.' He looked at her. 'Theodora is—Theodora. You'll know what I mean when you see her. She's rather difficult to describe,' he added unnecessarily.

'I gathered that,' she said drily. 'But I wouldn't have thought you, a writer, would be lost for words.'

He went through into the kitchen and began putting all the cleaning equipment down. Kim followed. 'The water's hot,' she said, 'or should be. I switched on the immersion heater when we came before. What about the others?'

'Butch is Ivan's bodyguard—of sorts. Built like an all-in wrestler, and about as thick as the proverbial two short planks—and Clinton is a designer—brilliant as a matter of fact, but not my cup of tea.' He paused. 'He and Theodora have a love–hate relationship—fireworks all round sometimes. It can get wearing.'

'Oh! I think I get the picture.' Kim tried to hide a smile, but didn't succeed.

'You will do when you meet them.' Luke switched on the hot tap.

'And Zara? Is she as beautiful as Ivan says?'

He shook his head. 'You'll have to see for yourself. He's had four wives—and she'll probably make the fifth. She's a fiery gipsy type—half Rumanian, the other half is anybody's guess, and her tongue can be sharp, but underneath she's probably got a heart of gold—though I wouldn't like to bet on it.'

Kim's heart sank. 'Oh. I see what you mean about being glad this cottage is here.'

'Yes.' He gave her a cool level glance. 'They have parties.' He let the last word sink in. 'I've been to one.' Another pause. 'I'm not sure what happened, but I didn't really surface for two days after.'

Kim swallowed. 'I think,' she said faintly, 'it's just as well Mr and Mrs Barnes are away. How long do you think they'll stay?'

He shrugged. 'Haven't a clue—although, knowing Ivan, he'll be wanting to move on in a few days.' He regarded her thoughtfully. 'There is one thing——'

Kim was intrigued, more by his hesitation than anything else. 'Yes?'

'Well, Zara is the—er—jealous type. And rather restless——' he paused again, and it seemed that he might be having difficulty in framing the words he wanted to say. 'If—er—she—thought——' he stopped.

Kim suddenly knew. 'Oh no,' she said firmly. 'Oh *no*!'

'How do you know what I was——'

'I'm not stupid,' she retorted. 'I'll *tell* you what you were going to say. If she thought I was making eyes at

Ivan—yes?' She waited.

'Well, it was just a thought——'

'Then I suggest you think again,' she said crisply. 'I have no intention of tangling with a she-cat—and in any case, why should she be jealous of *me*?' It was a loaded question, she realised that as soon as she had said it, but Luke's suggestion had been so preposterous that she had said the first thing that came into her head.

And there was a brief, pregnant silence. She was leaving herself wide open to a cutting answer. But Luke didn't. 'He likes you,' he answered.

It was not the reply she had expected, and in an odd way, she knew the truth of it. 'Yes,' she said quietly, 'I like him. In his outrageous way he's rather sweet.'

The moment had passed. 'Sweet?' Luke said, laughing. '*Sweet?* Ye gods, I've never heard him described like that before!'

Kim had gone pink. 'All right,' she said, 'laugh if you like. I know it sounds silly, but that's the way he struck me. So *there*!' It was a childish answer, but she didn't care.

Luke shrugged. 'Everyone to their own opinion, of course. Now, shall we get cracking?'

The cottage was looking spruce and tidy, the beds were made, and Luke had lit a wood fire in the living room which was crackling merrily—and he turned to Kim, who stood there squinting at a huge smut on her nose as she tried to wipe it off, and said: 'Here, let me.' As he did so the door opened, and Ivan walked in.

'Here you are!' he boomed. 'Come in, everyone, and meet Kim.' And in they came, two women, and two men, and the place erupted in laughter and noise, as Kim, bemused, well aware of her dishevelled appearance, tried to fathom out just who was who in that jazzy throng. The room was filled with colour. She had thought Ivan brightly dressed, but even he faded slightly in the profusion of reds, greens, golds and black of the women's apparel. Zara wore a dazzling kaftan of black and gold, and masses of gold jewellery about her neck, wrists and fingers. She was a striking redhead, with green eyes which sized Kim up in seconds, and she took her hand, murmured: 'So pleased to meet you,' in English even more fractured than Ivan's, and then embraced Luke warmly. 'Ah, Lukey my darlink,' she said, 'how lovely to see you again.'

Theodora—Kim knew what Luke meant, she did defy description—had short black hair, cut very angularly, with a fringe that came to a point on her forehead, flashing brown eyes, a brilliantly glossy red mouth—and a red denim boiler suit which almost hurt the eyes to see. The ensemble was completed by white cowboy boots—and a white blouse, dripping with lace, under the boiler suit. She too surveyed Kim shrewdly before greeting her. 'Hi,' she cried. 'What a cute little place you have—come and meet Kim, Clinton.'

By now Kim was wishing she had at least had a chance to wash before their arrival. She felt positively dowdy. Clinton was—there was no other way to describe him—a beautiful young man, tall, slim, with blond hair and blue eyes. The most conservatively dressed of the quartet, in a plain grey suit, he shook Kim's hand warmly. 'Hello,' he said, 'nice to meet you.'

Then she was introduced to Butch. He had waited quietly inside the door, and he had been watching her all along, and she knew that. His eyes were grey, flecked with green, and he was extremely tough-looking, with dark short hair, strong features, a battered nose—and a warm smile. 'Glad to meet you.'

Ivan beamed at them all. 'Now you all know each other,' he pronounced, satisfied. 'My children, I think we shall have a party to celebrate our arrival. Butch, the drinks are in the Rolls, here are the keys. And you, Theodora my poppet, shall fetch the food you have brought.' He turned to Luke and Kim. 'You will come along, yes?'

'Er—we have to get the guests' supper,' Luke answered, 'and we have to be up early——'

'Just for an hour or so! That is all. For your old friend Ivan you would not refuse, eh?' He looked like a child who had had a favourite toy taken from him. 'I insist—and in any case, Luke, we have business to discuss.'

'Well'—Luke looked at Kim—'just for an hour.'

'Good, good,' Ivan beamed. 'That is settled. Now, off you go and do whatever it is you have to do for those charming people at the hotel, and then return.' As they made their escape, laden with cleaning materials, his voice followed them: 'Bring them along too——'

They fled. Safely in the kitchen, Kim put her hand to her burning head. 'Oh dear,' she said, 'oh, *dear*!'

Luke looked grim. 'Okay, I know,' he said. 'Look, I'll go alone, if you don't want to. They're my responsibility, I realise that, and they are pretty overpowering——'

'It's all right,' said Kim. 'I wouldn't put it past Ivan to drag me out of bed—as long as it's only an hour.'

'It will be,' he answered. 'I'll make sure of that.' But it wasn't.

The three guests had had their suppers, Fiona had been fed, and had her walk, and everything was laid for breakfast, and Kim sat in the kitchen and wished she could creep away quietly to bed. Emma had telephoned from the hospital, and Kim had given her a carefully watered down version of the events of the day, then added that Ivan had paid in advance—a princely sum—for the use of the cottage, which news pleased Emma greatly, as she had known it would. Emma had heard enough to keep her going for a day or so, and Kim knew that she was under strain with Bill. And now, as she sat at the table and drank a glass of milk, she wished for nothing more than a quiet end to the day—which seemed a vain hope. In a minute she would have to go and find something chic to wear. But what? She had brought only severely practical clothes for her working holiday—and then she remembered Emma's wardrobe. They had had a good giggle when Kim had first arrived, over something that Bill had bought Emma for her birthday. 'He must think I'm a teenager,' Emma had said, producing a swirly, floating long dress in white chiffon, with gold braid at the low neckline. 'It's gorgeous—but I'll never dare wear it,' and she had sighed.

'Of course you will,' Kim had said enthusiastically. 'It suits everyone, a dress like this, and you just tie the cotton tape inside and gather it up—it fits any size too. Lucky you.' She remembered Emma's words. 'Well, love, if the prince arrives and asks you to the ball, you can borrow it.' They had laughed, the dress had been put away carefully in the wardrobe and forgotten. Emma would only be too pleased, Kim knew that, so her problem was solved. She would go and put it on, go to the party for one hour, no more, and then to bed.

She didn't see Luke as she ran upstairs to Emma's room. She heard the television from the lounge, and the voices, and she could guess the subject of conversation, for Ivan had introduced his little clan to the two sisters and the Colonel before departing for the cottage, and she could imagine the stunning effect that must have had. She grinned to herself as she lifted the dress from the wardrobe in Emma's room. If only Emma could imagine....

Fifteen minutes later she was ready. She twirled in front of her mirror, pleased with the dress. It flowed and swirled about her in filmy waves, and Emma's gold sandals fitted perfectly. 'Thanks, cousin,' she murmured, and went down to the kitchen.

He was waiting for her. As Kim went in the room, Luke stood up and looked at her. The tension which had been dispelled over the last few hours was suddenly back again, and she caught her breath. Now, just for the few brief minutes before they departed, they were alone. The air was charged with a sudden, subtle awareness, and a memory of what had once been. . . .

'Yes,' he said, and his voice was deep, 'I heard you getting ready.' The banal words did nothing to ease the atmosphere. It was as if they both knew, and remembered, and nothing would ever be the same again.

'I—borrowed a dress of Emma's,' Kim answered, trying desperately to speak in normal tones. 'I hadn't brought any.'

'It's fine. Shall we go?'

'Yes.' She could look at him now. 'We'll leave this light on.' He wore the white sweater over grey trousers. No jacket, nothing else, but there was an animal magnetism about him, an aura of strength and virility. He was all man, the spark of aggression she so well knew, all about him, and she suddenly thought: I'm going out into the dark night with him—and a shiver of apprehension touched her spine. He was stronger than any man she had ever met, and suddenly she was frightened.

'You go on,' she said. 'I'll follow in a—moment, I've just remembered——'

It was as if he knew. The throbbing silence filled the air, then: 'I'll wait. It's dark outside.'

'I—know.' Something must have showed in her eyes, for she heard his indrawn breath, saw his face change, darken, his eyes narrow.

'Oh *no*,' he said. 'What do you think I'm going to

do? Attack you? You must be——'

'Don't be silly!' she snapped, but he was there, holding her arm, and she felt stifled.

'Then why——'

'Let me go! I haven't——'

'You have. I can read it in your eyes. You're frightened of me, aren't you?'

'No, of course not!'

'I shan't touch you. Does that reassure you? Come on—the sooner we're there, the sooner we can leave.' And he took his hand from her arm, and turned away.

After a moment's hesitation Kim followed him towards the door. Luke opened it, took out the key and locked it on the outside. 'I'll keep this in my pocket,' he said. 'Okay?'

'Yes.' It was pitch black outside, and as the lights from the kitchen windows were left behind, and they were in the darkness of the trees, Kim's fears returned. Only a few minutes' walk to the cottage, yet it seemed an eternity, tall trees standing sentinel all around them, twigs and leaves crackling underfoot, the night air cool and scented, and the sound of music, growing gradually louder as they left the hotel behind and neared the cottage.

She stumbled, and he caught her by the elbow. 'Steady! I should have brought a torch. Can you see?'

'Yes—I—it was a branch or something.'

'We're nearly there. One hour, that's all we need to stay. They won't miss us when we leave,' he said, and he had kept his hand on her arm, but now she could see the lights blazing out from the cottage, and it rocked with the noise of the party—and she suddenly thought: I'm going to enjoy myself. And it was a surprising thought to have, because she had no idea at all, and she didn't really know any of them—and they were a rather overpowering bunch, *en masse*—and suddenly Kim began to laugh.

Luke stopped in his tracks. 'What the hell——' he began.

She stopped laughing. 'I don't know,' she admitted. 'I suddenly thought—I'm looking forward to it. Now isn't that *absurd*?'

'No.' He looked down at her, there in the shadowy darkness, with the light diffused in the night darkness, and his face was a grey blur. 'You could be right. Ivan exudes a kind of force, that affects all those around him. He can be hard—he's had to be, in his job—but he's childlike in a way, in his enjoyment of life, and in the fact that I've never known him do anything mean or underhand. I like and respect him—yes, I know I was trying to dodge him, but that was only because I knew damn well I'd not manage a scrap of writing with him around. I would like very much to sell him this book for filming.'

'Then you shall,' she said quietly. 'And with him at the cottage, it won't be so bad, you'll see.'

'I wish I had your confidence,' he said.

She looked sharply at him, searching for sarcasm, but could see none. She sobered, remembering all the other things between them, and now their relationship, of necessity, had to be impersonal—it was difficult, she knew that. Even more so that they were to be guests at Ivan's party, and Ivan clearly considered they were friends.

'Let's go in,' she said, and she sighed.

'Yes, we'd better.'

She thought she was drinking pineapple juice. It was only when she nearly fell over during a particularly riotous dance that Kim began to wonder what else her drink had been spiked with—and asked Ivan, as he re-filled her glass. 'Ah, my dear girl,' he chuckled, 'it is nothing—you are having a jolly time, yes?'

'Yes, lovely, but——' she hiccuped gently, 'but I'm feeling rather—oops!—woozy. Ivan——' she saw the half empty bottle of vodka nestling innocently on the table, looked round desperately, to see Luke doing a very efficient twist with Zara, knew she would get no support there—not for the moment anyway—and looked back at Ivan. 'You've been putting vodka in it, haven't you?' she accused.

'A drop only.' His face reflected his innocence, and she began to giggle helplessly.

'You're very, *very* bad,' she said firmly.

'I know. All my friends tell me. Come, dance—you will see me twist like no one has ever twisted before,' and he took her arm and whirled her on to the living room floor. He was right, no one could ever dance like him. The music was loud, the air was full of cigar smoke and perfume mingled, and everyone was having a riotous time.

Kim collapsed on to a chair after the dance, waving him away. 'That was lovely,' she sighed, 'but I'm go-

ing to close my eyes for five—five minutes.' And she
did. Only it wasn't for five minutes, it must have been
for more, because the next thing she knew she was in
her own bed.

# CHAPTER FIVE

KIM opened her eyes and could remember nothing—not even how she had got there. Then she turned her head, and saw the shadowy outline of a man by the window—and at the same moment as she realised that he was putting her dress over a chair, she also realised that she wore only bra and pants. She was instantly, devastatingly awake. She sat up, her breath catching in her throat, and he turned and saw her, there in the dim half light before morning comes, and moved towards her.

'Don't come any nearer,' she whispered. 'You undressed——'

'I took off your dress, yes,' he said. 'I've done it before—remember? Or perhaps you don't.' His voice was harsh. 'You were out like a light when I carried you back here. Would you rather I'd let you sleep in it?'

'How long have I been here?'

'Only a few minutes. Did you think I'd had time to rape you? You wouldn't have stayed asleep if I had, I promise you.'

'Get out.' She spoke in a low voice, devoid of expression, yet with all the force of her feelings hidden behind it. Luke looked at her, and it seemed that he knew, and she couldn't see his face, only the dark outline of him, tall, broad-shouldered, powerful—and she was afraid. Whether of him or herself she was not sure; she only remembered what had once been, and a treacherous weakness filled her, and was nearly overwhelming. And because of it she moved, flung the covers back, ready to go to the door, to make him leave, and her own heartbeats were deafening in her ears as she put her feet to the floor, stood up—and nearly fell as the effects of the vodka she had unknowingly drunk hit her forcefully.

Luke caught her. 'Steady,' he said, 'you're as drunk as a——'

'Take your hands off me!' she breathed. 'Take——'

'Do you think I want to touch you? My God, I'd have to be desperate for a woman before I'd——'

She struggled free, and hit him hard, and the room spun round with the effort and she wanted to cry out, but couldn't, and he caught her again and pushed her back on the bed. 'You little fool,' he said, and his voice was deep and husky, 'don't you know there are rooms underneath? Do you want everyone——'

'I don't care—get *out*!' but she was helpless in a grip of steel, and his body was beside her, across the bed, and she wasn't sure how it had happened, whether he had fallen or was merely holding her to stop her escaping; then she felt the warmth of him, and sensed his sudden excitement and anger mingled, and she was struggling, wriggling, trying to free herself, only it seemed to be having an effect on him that she dimly realised was the opposite of what she intended. Or was it? Her head reeled, yet her body moved of its own volition nearer to him. Then he kissed her ... and she hated herself for her response, because she hated him, and yet at the same time she remembered that look she had seen on his face, the look of a man who had once loved her—deeply. His lips were hot and searching, and her mind, now totally confused, was not important; only the sensations mattered, the urgent hard caresses, Luke's hands moving freely, her skin responding to the touch she had once known so well, her whole body aching at the memories that flared in a sudden rush of desire.

'No! I hate—you—I——' she whispered, while her body said differently.

'And I hate you,' he said huskily, 'but it's not going to stop me. Nothing is——' his lips traced a path down her cheek, her throat, to her breast. And he said again: 'Nothing——' and then there were no more words, only a savage, punishing lovemaking that went on for ever....

Kim awoke, and looked to the pillow beside her, but Luke had gone. She closed her eyes again, reliving what had happened, and her whole body ached with the memory of it, and she stirred and moaned softly, and put her hand to her burning lips. Nothing before, during the brief time they were married, had ever been like that. And nothing would ever be the same again. She got shakily out of bed and went over to the mirror, and it reflected her nakedness as she looked at herself, and saw her eyes, wide and dark, staring back at her. There was a bruise on her arm, and beneath her neck. She touched them gently, and winced. Then, turning away, she pulled on her dressing gown and went to have a bath.

It was nearly eight-thirty. She bathed quickly, cleansing the memories away, dressed and went downstairs. The back door was open, and somewhere outside Fiona barked. Then Luke came out of the pantry and closed the door behind him. Kim's heart leapt. She hadn't been prepared for this. She wanted only time alone, to think, to drink a coffee——

He looked the same as ever. Fully dressed, perhaps a little tired round the eyes, that was the only difference. 'Sleep well?' he enquired mockingly. Kim didn't answer. She went to the stove, saw that the kettle was nearly boiling, and put some instant coffee in a cup. Underneath, on the grill, bacon sizzled appetisingly, and bread was stacked at the side of the toaster, waiting, and at the back of the stove was a huge pan of fat succulent sausages. 'It's nearly ready,' he said, 'as you can see.'

She made her coffee, adding plenty of cold milk. And then she looked at him, and she didn't try to hide what was in her eyes. He met her gaze steadily, unblinking. 'You asked for it,' he said. 'And you got it.' A muscle moved in his jaw. 'I'll bet Paul was never that good, eh?'

Kim didn't stop to think what she was doing, it was a reflex action, born of humiliation. She flung the coffee all over him, saw it pouring down his face and sweater with a faint, ghastly feeling inside her—then Luke moved like lightning, caught her, and held her, and shook her. She had never seen such anger in anyone. For a moment she thought he was going to beat her, so savagely did he hold her. Then he spoke, his voice low and controlled with fury. 'You'll be sorry you did that,' he said, and flung her away from him. He put his hand up to wipe his face.

Shaken, she leaned against the dresser, feeling the hard ledge behind her.

'I won't let you get near me again,' she gasped. 'You'll never get the chance!'

'Won't I? I wouldn't be too sure of that if I were you——' he broke off as Fiona came in, wagging her tail at Kim in greeting. 'I'm going to change. You'd better get the toast going. And don't forget what I said.' And he smiled, then went out. Kim stared after him, unable to move. The smile had chilled her blood. The awful thing was, she knew precisely what it meant. If he had been going to hit her, he would have done so then, in his fury. He would find another way to punish her, and she knew full well what it was, and she wasn't sure if she could bear it.

She began to make the toast for the guests' breakfast. There was work to be done, and later, phone calls to make, to see how the Barnes' were, and to tell Emma that everything was running smoothly. A laugh caught in her throat. Smoothly—oh yes, it was that all right. No complaints from the guests, and food cooked properly and on time, and the cottage let for a very nice sum of money to a crowd of extroverts who might possibly, if Ivan Zolto liked Luke's book, bring a a lot more money to the hotel. Which was just what Emma and Bill needed. And I came here to help, she thought, as she watched the toaster pop up and deftly put the pieces to keep warm under the bacon before putting four more slices in, and I am helping—perhaps a little more than was intended, because of the Barnes' illness, but then Luke's pulling his weight as well—in between raping me—and so everything on the surface is normal. And when I leave here I should be cured of him—perhaps of all men—for ever. 'Dear God,' she put her hand to her eyes to wipe away the welling tears, 'what have I done?'

The door slammed, and Luke was in the kitchen, filling it with an unbearable tension. Kim must have spoken aloud, for she heard his laugh as he strode over. 'That's a question you should ask yourself in the still watches of the night, when you're alone,' he said. He had changed into a dark blue sweater and flung the coffee-stained one at her. 'That needs washing,' he said.

She put it to one side and looked at him. From her despair had come a kind of strength. 'I shall be doing a wash later,' she said. 'Shall I serve breakfast, or will you?'

'I'll do it. Set out the plates.' Then there was no time for talk as the first real job of the day was done. For the next fifteen minutes, Kim had no time to think either, only do the essentials, the toast, the coffee and the tea while Luke vanished and reappeared for more plates.

Then came the calm. All that remained now was to snatch a bite herself, and wait for their three guests to finish eating, then go in and clear away. She didn't feel hungry at all. Luke made himself a sandwich of bacon and sausages and sat at the table. Kim picked up his sweater. 'I'm going to do the wash,' she said.

'And I'm going over to Ivan's to see if they need any food or booze. I'm driving down to the village later. You'd better make a list of what we need.' His voice was normal, as though nothing had happened. Perhaps he would forget. . . .

'Right, I will.' She kept her voice as calm as his. 'If you could look in on the Barnes' and enquire how soon they'll be back—it will save me ringing.'

He nodded. 'Put it at the top of your list, then I won't forget.' And just as he finished speaking, the telephone shrilled. Kim looked at him.

'Shall I——?' she began.

'No, I will.' He picked it up. 'Good morning, Rykin Hotel.' The accent, she realised, was Scottish again, not unpleasant, and quite decidedly unlike his own. And she knew who was calling by the way he stiffened, the way he spoke. She wanted to laugh and cry at the same time. Was it his mistress? The thought was almost amusing. He was a man who would need a woman; she had known that when she married him so briefly three years ago, and had had it even more forcibly demonstrated only hours previously. His physical needs were strong, and yet there had been something in the desperate savagery with which he had made love to her. That she only now remembered, as she heard him, as if from a distance, talking, evading . . . . He had been like a man who had not made love for a very long time. . . .

'Ding!' The telephone crashed back onto the receiver with a bang, and he turned away, furious, she could tell. That again was almost funny.

'Oh dear,' she said. 'Was it your lady friend again?'

Luke swore softly under his breath, then turned towards her. 'I'm glad you find it so hilarious,' he said.

'I'm sorry.' She assumed a contrite expression. At least his anger wasn't directed at her for once. 'Wouldn't it have been better if I'd answered?'

'You didn't do so well the first time,' he responded.

'Well, is she coming here or not?'

His glance was stony. 'I shouldn't be at all surprised.'

'Then hadn't you better describe her? I can watch out for her and tell her we're full up. And incidentally, hadn't you better hide your car? Ivan recognised it.' She was surprised at how calm and reasonable her voice sounded.

'She's a bit taller than you, blonde short hair, very slim, tanned face, rather full mouth—and her name's Gail Henderson.'

Kim smiled. 'I can remember. Er—it's no business of mine, but why don't you want to see her? She sounds very attractive.'

'You're right, it is no business of yours, but I'll tell you anyway. She's an actress, and she'd desperately love a part in this film, and if she had any idea that Ivan was here, nothing, but nothing, would keep her away.'

'I see. Her voice—last time—sounded more personal than that—as if she were a very good friend of yours.' Kim's tone was totally innocent. She began to feel much better than she had before, but she didn't understand why.

'She's an actress, remember? She can make it sound how she likes.'

'Oh. Then you're not having an affair with her?' She didn't know why she had said it. She couldn't explain it, it was as though her words were being spoken by another person. Faintly horrified, Kim heard herself say them, and waited for his reaction.

'I've been out with her a few times. That doesn't constitute an affair.' She was treading on dangerous ground. She knew she was, but she couldn't stop herself.

'She's a woman, isn't she?' she retorted. 'I would have thought *that* was enough for you———'

'Why don't you shut up?' His eyes glinted darkly, his face was suddenly drawn.

Kim widened her eyes. 'Oh dear! How tactless of me! She said no, did she?' She turned away because she didn't really know what had got into her, and marched out to the laundry room. Luke followed her and slammed shut the door behind him.

'And what do you mean by that?' He leaned against the door, all six feet three of him, and there was no escape.

'Nothing,' she muttered, and began to pile sheets and tablecloths into the washing machine. Next moment she was grabbed by the arm and swung round to face him.

'Don't turn away when I'm talking to you,' he gritted.

'Ouch! Let me go—you're hurting me!'

'Not as much as I would like to.' He looked down at her, looked at her heaving breast inside the thin white sweater she wore, then back at her face. 'And I can hurt you, make no mistake about that.'

'You already did, just a short while ago.' Her voice trembled at the memory, and at her own treachery. She took a deep, shaky breath. 'But at least, if she came here, you might leave me alone.'

His eyes bored into hers, as if daring her to look away. 'It wouldn't be any fun—with her,' he said softly, 'but with you——' he stopped, the words unspoken, then he ran his tongue over his lips. 'With you it's different.'

Kim couldn't breathe. She wanted to scream, but no sound would come. And her arms and legs had gone weak, so weak that she would have fallen had he not held her so strongly. 'No——' she whispered. It was all she could manage. 'Please—not again—not here——'

'Yes. Again—and here. I'm going to take you now.'

She knew why she had said what she had. Because, deep inside herself, she had known what would happen as a result, and as his mouth came down on hers in a savage searing kiss it was just like before, only——

'No.' He moved slightly away from her, and looked at her, and shook his head. 'You're right—not here.' Kim closed her eyes, because she could not bear to see the knowledge in his—because he knew. Luke laughed. 'Later,' he said. 'I'm going to see Ivan now. Get your washing done, and your list made. I'll be back later for it.' As he walked away from her, out of the room, he began to laugh again. Kim put her knuckles to her mouth and pressed hard. She heard again his mocking laughter, and the taunting, ambiguous words: 'I'll be back later for it.' And she knew, with an odd kind of instinct, that her punishment had only just begun. Yet it was so different later, when Ivan and his cronies came over in the afternoon and all trooped into the kitchen as though they belonged there, and indeed, thought Kim dazedly, it was almost as if they did. Clinton and Theodora draped themselves over chairs and continued a mild bickering that had obviously been going on for some time, Butch sat in a corner and stroked a besotted Fiona and watched Kim's every move, while Ivan and Zara came over to the cooker and looked at Kim, and Zara said: 'We have come to help you,' in her delightful fractured English. Luke, busily pouring out the wine they had brought over, looked up.

'That's very kind of you, Zara,' he said. 'Here, have some wine,' and handed her a glass. 'But I think Kim has everything under control, haven't you, Kim?'

'Yes, perfectly,' she answered. 'In fact I'm making soup—and there'll be enough for you all if you'd like some.'

Ivan's face fell. 'You need no help?' he boomed sadly. 'But we would like———'

'You see, Ivan old chap,' said Luke in very matey tones,' it's just that Kim and I have worked out a routine'—oh, haven't we just, thought Kim sourly—'and while we appreciate everything, you can understand that too many cooks spoil the broth.'

Ivan frowned. 'But we have not yet touched the broth.'

You need a sense of humour with this crowd, thought Kim desperately. And I'm not even sure if I've got one any more, after all that's happened. She continued stirring as Theodora's explanations of old English proverbs, and what Luke had really meant, washed over and around her. Then someone pushed a glass of wine into her hand and she turned to thank them, and saw Butch smiling at her. 'Seeing as you're the only one doing any work,' he said, 'you might as well have a drink.'

'Why, thank you.' She sipped. It was cool, and very dry and pleasant. They were in a little oasis of quiet amid the other raised voices, everyone talking at once, proverbs being hurled back and forth, and explanations. Butch just looked at her, and she thought—he fancies me, and it was rather a sad thought, because although she liked him instinctively, she didn't fancy him in any way. Then, glancing across the room, she saw Luke pause in what he was saying and look at them, and for a moment she caught a glimpse of something puzzling on his face. Something she didn't understand.

She smiled brightly at Butch. 'The wine is lovely. But I mustn't drink too much. I have work to do.'

'Anything I can help with?' For a moment she was tempted to say, yes, you can give my ex-husband a good hiding—but the temptation was resisted.

'Nothing, thanks. As Luke says, it's all organised. Besides, you're a guest.'

'I'm working too, as Ivan's bodyguard. Have you ever seen a man who needs one less?'

She laughed. 'Not really. Do you like your work?'

He shrugged. 'I see the world, stay in all the best places, and I like him very much. Yes, I like my work.'

'Have you ever been in one of Ivan's films?' She regretted the question instantly as she saw what she saw in his eyes. Then it was gone.

'No.'

Something made her say: 'I'm sorry.'

He smiled. 'Why?'

'Because—forgive me—I thought you might want to——'

'You're very perceptive.' He gave her a wry smile. 'I'm just "good old Butch", you know—not considered very bright.'

'Don't be ridiculous!' Kim remembered Luke's description of him as being thick. Perhaps that was what everyone thought, but she knew they were wrong.

Butch laughed then, without any bitterness. 'Thanks.'

'I didn't mean to be insulting,' she explained hastily. 'You underestimate yourself.'

'I know you weren't being. And perhaps I do. Only when you're built like me they assume it's a case of all brawn and no brain.'

'In the same way as everyone considers beauty queens empty-headed?' she nodded. 'I know what you mean.'

'Something like that. And I've got a darned good job, so——' he shrugged, 'why should I worry?'

'As long as you're happy.' But an idea was stirring at the back of her mind. Butch would like to act. She had seen that before he could wipe it away. And Ivan liked her. Kim smiled a little smile to herself. He might listen—when the time came....

'You're smiling,' he said.

'Just a thought.' She looked at him again. But she couldn't tell him, not yet. 'I was just thinking how nice it is to talk to you.'

His face softened. 'Can't you talk to Luke?' The conversation eddied round them, no one was listening at all. She sensed an ally—and she desperately needed someone to talk to.

'I was married to him once,' she said softly. 'And neither of us knew the other was coming here—does that answer your question?'

'My God!' He looked at her sadly. 'I'm sorry, Kim.'

'It was all over three years ago,' she said. 'It was just unfortunate that we both arrived—me to help my cousin—on the the same day. I even crashed my car into his on the way here.'

'You weren't hurt?'

'No. It was a minor bump, that's all——' she paused. 'I don't know why I'm telling you my troubles. Please, don't say anything. No one else knows.' She looked anxiously at him, and saw by his face that she could trust him.

'I won't. You have my word on that.' He glanced across at Luke, who was trying to get plates out of a cupboard while conducting a lively conversation with

Zara and Clinton. 'And did he come here to work as well?'

'No. But the cook and her husband are ill, so he volunteered. I must be honest, I don't know how I'd have managed without him.'

'I liked him,' Butch said thoughtfully.

Alarm flared. 'Please, don't stop liking him because I've told you what I did.'

He laughed. 'All right, I'll try. But I'd like to bash his head in for him!'

It was said with such a boyish frankness that she too laughed. 'I hope you're joking——'

'Yes—partly. Okay Kim, relax. Of course I'm kidding.' He put his hand on her arm briefly. 'I'd better go now. I've got to see that teacher lady later—what's her name?'

'Miss Dines?'

'That's the one. She asked me if I'd move her wardrobe for her—didn't want to bother you 'cos she knows you're busy'—oh boy, thought Kim, after one look at you, I'll bet she didn't—'so I'm seeing her after dinner.'

'Hmm,' said Kim. 'I *see*.'

'Meaning?' But he guessed as he said it.

'Oh, nothing. I'm sure you can take care of yourself. You're a big boy.'

'It's all right—but thanks for the subtle warning anyway. I can act very dumb when I want, you know.'

She grinned. There was something very appealing about Butch, something very likeable. 'Let me know how you go on.'

'Yes, I will. Do you still love him?' The question was so unexpected that she dropped the soup ladle with a clatter. No one looked round.

'What?'

'I said—no, never mind. It's none of my business.'

Kim was busy wiping the ladle after rinsing it under the tap. 'The answer is—no, I don't.' She stared at him defiantly, as if daring him to contradict her, and he raised his hands in a gesture of surrender.

'Okay—sorry. I just thought—if you wanted to—er —make him jealous, perhaps I could help.'

'That's quite ridiculous——' she started to smile. What a thought! 'No,' she shook her head. 'Thanks anyway, but——'

'Yes, well, the offer's open if you need it. Must go now. I'm driving to the village for some drink for Ivan. Need anything?'

'No, thanks, Butch. We'll have another chat some time.'

'You can bet on it!' He smiled and left her to thread his way through the crowded kitchen to Ivan, then went out.

The next two hours were hectic, and gave Kim little time to think about anything but cooking dinner. Somehow, she wasn't sure how it had happened, but Ivan and his friends had decided they would like to sample her cooking, and would stay for dinner, and Theodora found herself an apron, shooed everyone out, and said she would help. Ivan persuaded Luke to go off to some remote corner of the hotel and discuss the book, Zara and Clinton hovered for a few minutes wondering if anything needed doing, rather vaguely, and were sent off with instructions to entertain the two schoolteachers, and Kim and Theodora were at last alone, and able to get on with what they were doing.

'There now,' said Theodora, looking round her with satisfaction after checking potatoes and vegetables and roast ducklings and doing a dozen other jobs in quick firefly succession that left Kim agape with admiration. 'All is under control, I think, so sit down, love, and we'll have a glass of wine.'

Kim, bemused, did as she was told. 'You wouldn't like a job here, would you?' she asked wistfully.

Theodora threw back her head and laughed heartily. 'My parents have a very busy café in London, ducky, and I'm pure cockney—though I can put on any accent I choose—and on the rare occasions I get back there for a weekend I put on me old pinny and get right behind that counter—I love it.' She stretched herself gloriously, like a sleek cat. 'And one day, when I'm old and grey, I'm going to run a hotel just like this one and have a dozen cats and be a contented old lady.'

'You'll never be old,' Kim laughed.

'Probably not, but it's nice to have a dream of your own. I live in a world where we manufacture dreams, don't forget, until you're never sure where the real world ends and fantasy begins.' She shrugged. 'I've seen it all, met all the stars, the great ones and the ones who'll never make it—and you can spot the difference right away.' She finished her wine. 'Stop me if I'm boring you.'

'I'm fascinated,' Kim said with truth.

'You are? No kidding? Perhaps I'll write a book about it some day.' Theodora got to her feet. 'Work to be done. We'll have a talk some time and I'll tell you some things about the famous film stars'—she waved her hand—'oh boy! you wouldn't *believe*. Phew!' She darted off to the stove, laughing, and Kim followed. Then Luke came in alone, and the atmosphere changed. Theodora seemed unaware of it, yet Kim suspected she was very shrewd and chose to ignore it. 'Hi,' she said brightly. 'Just in time. Is everyone in the dining room?'

'Yes. I've come to help.'

'Well, just stand aside and you can in one moment. Kim, dish out the soup and Luke can take it in while I carve the duckling.' She was busy as she spoke and within minutes everything was ready to be whisked in after the soup was finished.

When at last it was all done, Kim and Theodora sat down to eat their meal belatedly, and Theodora gave Kim a very old-fashioned look and said: 'And what gives with you two?'

It would be no good being evasive with her. 'I thought you'd noticed something,' Kim answered. She shrugged. 'We don't get on very well.' Which was a massive understatement, considering everything.

'Yeah. He brought in his own icicles with him—and I saw him look at you.'

'You don't miss much, do you?'

'No,' admitted Theodora, unabashed. 'But then I saw his face before, when you and Butch were having that heart-to-heart over a hot stove——'

'And?' Kim stared at her as she gave a reflective smile.

'Why, ducky, he looked as jealous as *hell*!'

Now that *was* funny, and Theodora was well off beam. 'Oh no,' gasped Kim, amused, 'sorry, but you're mistaken.'

'I'm never mistaken,' said Theodora with great confidence. 'Not in things like that.' Kim stared at her, and her smile slowly vanished. She was rapidly revising her opinion of what she had thought of as a bunch of colourful eccentrics.

'Oh,' said Kim, because she couldn't say anything else at that moment.

'Interesting, very interesting,' Theodora drawled the words, and gave Kim a charming elfin grin. 'Don't mind me, love, I just adore fireworks.'

'But——'

'Let it all happen. Luke is a very sexy gentleman—or hadn't you noticed?'

Oh, I'd noticed all right, Kim thought. She sighed. Today was confession day, it seemed. 'We were once married,' she said. 'Very secretly—and very briefly. But we both came here by chance.'

Theodora's eyes widened. 'Wow! What a story! Honestly?'

'Yes, honestly. I told Butch—now I'm telling you. I don't know what's come over me, Theodora, I seem to be going round telling everybody——' and she burst into tears.

'There now, love, it's all right, don't cry—here——'

a man's handkerchief was pushed into her hand. 'It's clean. Blow your nose and wipe your eyes. Men! Sometimes I'd like to strangle them all——' Theodora stopped as Luke came in, and she turned to him. 'Not now, Luke love, if you don't mind. Why don't you go and help Butch shift the old dragon's wardrobe—Kim and I are having a girl-talk.' And Kim heard the door slam. He hadn't said a word. 'He's gone,' said Theodora, unnecessarily. 'He didn't look very pleased. Still, I don't suppose he likes being told what to do—none of them do. Arrogant beast!' She pulled a chair up next to Kim's and poured her a cup of coffee from the pot. 'Drink that, and tell me *all*—or as much as you want to. I'm a good listener.' She watched Kim sip the hot coffee. 'That's it. Do you good. Then I'll tell you my little plan.'

'Plan?' Kim croaked. 'What do you——'

'Ssh! You first, me later.' So Kim sketched in, very briefly, the picture of her and Luke, and what had happened, and Theodora listened patiently and carefully to it all. Kim didn't tell her everything because she couldn't tell anyone *that*—but she told her enough.

'Right,' said Theodora, when Kim had done. 'Now I'll tell *you* something. He needs teaching a lesson, that one. And I'm going to help you do it. Then we'll see whether I was right or not about him being jealous.' She started to talk, and Kim listened. . . .

# CHAPTER SIX

'GIVE me strength,' sighed Luke. 'They'll have you as nutty as they are soon, if you're not careful.'

'*I* think they're very nice—all of them,' retorted Kim with great calm. They were preparing supper in the kitchen, and from far away in the lounge came great sounds of merriment and an accordion being played at its loudest. Everyone was there, even the Colonel. The drink had flowed freely all evening and she wasn't sure if anyone would want coffee, but she had come out to make it, and Luke had followed her. Kim had drunk very little herself. She wanted a clear head at all times. There would be no repetition of last night. 'And in any case, who's responsible for them being here? Not me.' She turned her back on him and began to set out the tray.

'And was it your idea that Butch should move in here?' he said harshly.

She turned to face him. 'No. Theodora's. Poor Butch had been sleeping on a settee in the cottage, she said. It seemed charitable—we do have the beds, after all.'

'He's supposed to stay near Ivan——' he began. Kim laughed merrily.

'He doesn't need a bodyguard *here* any more than you do, and you know it. Are you going to carry in the tray? I'll get the petits fours out of the pantry. Theodora made them earlier. Mind you,' she added thought-fully, 'he'll probably need one if your Gail Henderson arrives—but we'll wait until that happens.'

Luke suddenly took hold of her and turned her to face him. She stared at him defiantly. 'Listen,' he said, his voice low and harsh, 'you are severely trying my patience with your flip attitude——'

'You're hurting me,' she said quietly. 'Why don't you try grabbing hold of someone nearer your size— say Butch—and see where that gets you?'

He smiled thinly. 'He doesn't frighten me—is that the idea? Why he's here? I thought you'd be more original than that.'

'I like him, as a matter of fact.'

'Yes—and I'll bet he likes you. But there's only one thing he'd want.'

'And you'd know all about that, wouldn't you?' she retorted evenly. Then Butch walked in as she said it, almost as if on cue.

Luke merely turned his head. 'We're managing without help, thanks,' he said. 'And guests aren't sup-posed to come into the kitchens.'

'Kim invited me, didn't you, Kim?' said Butch goodhumouredly. 'Having trouble?'

'Nothing I can't cope with.' She pushed Luke away from her and went to the table, trying to hide the trembling of her limbs. She could feel the tension building up to a fine sharp pitch, and she was dis-turbed, because suddenly, in that moment of Butch's entry, she had known the truth. She didn't want either of them hurt. Butch, because she liked him—Luke, be-

# What secrets lie within the Hotel De La Marine?

For weeks the small French fishing village of Port Royal had been aflame with rumors about the mysterious stranger. Why had he come? What was he after? Challenged by his haughty, yet haunted demeanor, Marie was determined to break through his mask of indifference. But he was as charming as he was cunning, uncanny in perception and driven by vengeance. From the moment she learned his secret, Marie lived with the fear of discovery, and the thrill of danger.

Uncover those secrets with Marie in the gripping pages of *High Wind in Brittany* by *Caroline Gayet*—one of the many best-selling authors of romantic suspense presented by Mystique Books.

# MYSTIQUES

Now every month you can be spellbound by 4 exciting Mystique novels like these. You'll be swept away to casinos in Monte Carlo, ski chalets in the Alps, or mysterious ruins in Mexico. You'll experience the excitement of intrigue and the warmth of romance. Mystique novels are all written by internationally acclaimed, best-selling authors of romantic suspense.

Subscribe now! As a member of the Mystiques Subscription plan, you'll receive 4 books each month. Cancel anytime. And still keep your 4 FREE BOOKS!

cause he was the man she loved. And one wrong word, one wrong gesture on her part could trigger off a fight. It had seemed so harmless, almost amusing, when they had talked of it. The reality was different. Two men, both strong and tough, were poised on a knife edge of aggression for their own different reasons, and she was in the middle of it.

She looked from one to the other, seeing the way they stood, the tautness of their features. One word, that was all. She took a deep breath, then—'Oh! What was *that*?' She flew to the kitchen door, flung it open and stared at them both. 'I saw someone——'

They both ran out and Kim collapsed against the sink in relief. Luke came back first. 'Very clever,' he said softly.

'I don't know what you mean——' then as Butch came in, 'Did you see him?'

'No. No one out there.'

'Oh! Thank heavens.' Kim gave a delicious shudder. 'I thought I saw a face at the window. It must have been the ghost. Butch, will you carry in the tray?' She handed it to him before he could say yes or no and give him a lovely smile. 'Luke will bring in the coffee in a minute.' She held the door open for him and whispered as he passed: 'It's okay. I'll be in in a moment.'

The coffee was ready. She looked at Luke—the man she had suddenly realised she had never stopped loving—and said: 'It's done.'

'Are you the peacemaker?'

'I didn't want you getting hurt,' she answered crisply.

'Me—or him?'

'Both.'

'Then you did a clever move. You're to be congratulated. Because there was about to be one hell of a fight.'

'I know that. Fights don't solve anything, do they?'

'It all depends,' he shrugged.

'On what?'

'Circumstances.'

'You talk in riddles,' she said. 'Are you taking in the coffee or not?'

'I'll take it—when we've finished our talk.'

'Don't start that again,' she said wearily. 'There's nothing to talk about. We're here. We're working. We're not married. That says it all.'

'I forgot to tell you—I don't believe in divorce.'

'You left it a bit late in the day to tell me that, didn't you?' She stared at him. 'Is that why you raped me?'

'It wasn't rape,' he said flatly. 'And it won't be next time.'

'There won't be a next time.'

'Won't there?' he smiled. 'That should make it more interesting. More of a challange.'

'I've a very good lock on my door.'

'And I have the master key.'

Kim stared at him. She had never thought of that. A strange excitement filled her. 'You have no right——' she began, and stopped.

'Perhaps not,' he smiled. 'So what are you going to do about it?'

She picked up the coffee pot without a word, and marched out. She would think of something, even if it meant dragging her dressing table to block the door. She thought about it when she poured out the coffee and made small talk for the benefit of the party in the lounge. Whatever happened, Luke would not get into her room, ever again; on that she was decided.

The party over, washing up done, Luke over at the cottage talking, Kim had a last look round the kitchen, patted Fiona, switched out the light and went up the stairs to her room. She didn't want to make too much noise dragging furniture about, so she would block the door handle with a chair, that was easiest. She washed in her own tiny attic bathroom, unlocked her door and went in, locking it after her. Then she switched on the light, and Luke stood up from his chair by the window, and said: 'Surprise, surprise,' and walked over to her. 'Now about that coffee you threw over me this morning,' he added. He put his arms round her and drew her towards him.

Kim, too stunned to speak at first, began to struggle, tried to speak, but his lips crushed hers, and she was silent. His hands moved silently, caressingly, then he picked her up and carried her over to the bed, pulled her down, crushing her body with his, and she heard his fierce words: 'Why aren't you fighting me?'

How could she answer that truthfully? How could she say what she knew inside her—that this was all she had ever wanted? She began to struggle, pushing him, lashing out at him, writhing away, and she knew his excitement was growing, as was her own desire; then it didn't matter any more....

She awoke, and Luke was there beside her, and she knew he was awake too. The darkness was outside, the room was shadowy and cool, and everywhere was silent and still. She was aware of him so strongly that it overwhelmed her. He had made love to her out of hate, of punishment, but it took nothing away. She had abandoned herself completely to his stormy violence, matching it with her own, until, exhausted, they had slept. Now she looked at him, through half closed eyes, keeping her breathing deep and steady so that he should not know she had awoken, and he stirred and turned slightly, his arm sliding across her naked body, and she sighed as though in sleep and half turned also so that she was on her back. Closing her eyes, waiting.... And now, this time, was the most beautiful of all, a slow leisurely wandering through the gates of desire, a rich fulfilling time that left her utterly and completely exhausted. It was silent, no words were said, no struggles, just an all-consuming fire that swept them both along to its shattering climax.

She slept, after, a deep dreamless sleep, and she knew she would never love any other man as long as she lived. When she opened her eyes again it was morning, and a deep shame, almost a sense of revulsion filled her as she remembered all that had happened. It couldn't go on. For the sake of her own pride—what was left of it—she must not allow it to happen again.

She dragged herself out of bed and went to the window. She had been asleep when he left, and yet a memory stirred, and was gone, and it seemed that she had dreamed it, dreamed of Luke kissing her as he left her, a mere butterfly touch on the cheek that spoke more than any words could have—but it was a dream, of course, for he hated her, he used her purely to satisfy his animal needs. She shuddered now at the memory, and the shame, and knew that in a day or so, when the Barnes' were back, and he was once again elevated to the status of guest, and engrossed with Ivan and company, all would be over. She washed and dressed quickly, and had a feeling of relief that all would work out. Soon he would leave too, and she would go back to her job in London, and it would be an episode that passed. But she would never forget him, that was the only difference.

Today was now, was all that counted, and there was work to be done. It would all go smoothly, provided she hardened her heart.... Only it didn't work out quite like that, and it started to go awry immediately after breakfast....

The first thing was the telephone call from Emma's Aunt Jessie to say could the children come home at once because her next door neighbour's husband had had a stroke and the next door neighbour needed help and comforting, and anyway Aunt Jessie was seventy-one and hadn't realised just how tiring a healthy active twelve-year-old girl and ten-year-old boy could be, and much as she loved them she'd had enough, and for another thing they were missing their parents—and to cut a long story short, now that Kim was there it would be lovely because they thought the world of her, and she, Aunt Jessie, who was Bill's aunt really, was looking forward to meeting her one day—Kim managed to cut short the flow of oratory, promised to have them met off the noon train, thanked Aunt Jessie profusely, and fled to the kitchen—where she bumped into Luke, who was just coming out.

'Oh!' she glared at him helplessly, pushed past him and went over to the sink and banged a few dishes about. She loved Caroline and Mark too, but they certainly wouldn't simplify matters. That's all I need, she thought. The sooner the Barnes' are back, the better. Only that was the next telephone call, from Mrs Barnes, to say that the doctor refused to sign them off and it would have to be another week.... Kim reeled from that shock straight into the arms of Butch who had brought an armful of empty bottles out from the lounge. He rescued one bottle as it toppled, set them on the table, and said:

'What's up, love?'

She told him, her face showing her feelings. He touched her arm. 'I'll meet the kids,' he said. 'Ivan will lend me the car. And I'll do the jobs Mr—what's the name? Barnes? does—so what's the problem?'

She sniffed. 'You make it sound so easy,' she shook her head. 'Thanks, Butch.'

'Okay. Now sit down, I'll make you a coffee. You're working too hard—I'll have a word with Thea, she likes cooking. That big swine Luke can go and get lost—you'll see.'

'There are two more guests arriving tomorrow,' she said, 'as well.'

'So? What's two more? Cheer up, Kim——'

'You're smashing,' she interrupted.

'I know.' He gave a modest sigh.

'And you make me laugh!'

'Not all the time, I hope.' He picked up the bottles to carry them out, and gave her a look. When he came back he made two coffees, pulled up a chair, and sat down. 'Okay, describe the kids—better give me a note. They won't know me from Adam.'

'Yes, I will.' There came a loud ring from the reception desk in the hall, and Kim jumped. Had she got the day wrong? Was that the Ellisons?

Butch stood up. 'Stay there, I'll get it,' and he went out. But Kim followed him, saw him vanish, and scampered after him to see him talking to a stunning blonde in the hall.

'Oh!' She darted back into the shelter of the corridor, heart beating fast. Even if Luke hadn't described Gail, she would have guessed. She put her hand to her mouth to stifle a giggle. What on earth did she do now? She didn't need to do anything, for she heard the voices—then Luke's—Gail's delighted squeak—and the next moment, Butch came hurrying back, nearly knocking her over. He took one look at Kim, half lifted her, and carried her into the kitchen, where he slammed the door shut and burst out laughing.

'That's Luke's girl-friend,' he said, when he could speak.

A totally unexpected pang of jealousy shot through Kim. She took a deep breath. 'I know—she's been phoning and I've been putting her off.'

'It's too late now. She attached herself to him like a limpet the moment she saw him.' He gave her an odd look. 'Things are certainly happening today, aren't they?'

She swallowed the coffee, which was too sweet and strong, but precisely what she needed. 'I suppose I'd better go and see——' she began, then stopped. 'No, let *him* sort her out.'

'You mean he really doesn't want her here?'

'No.' She glared at him, not sure why that should annoy her.

'Okay, sorry,' he grinned. 'Don't shout, I only *asked*.'

'She's an actress—she wants a part in this film— *any* film,' Kim explained.

'I though she looked familiar.' He gave a low whistle. 'Wait till she finds out Ivan's here.'

'Precisely,' answered Kim crisply.

'And then wait until Zara sees her.' He smiled reflectively. 'Mmm, yes.'

'Meaning?'

'You'll see.' He stood up. 'Write me a note, love, and I'll go and tell Ivan about the car and warn him about —what's her name?'

'Gail Henderson.'

'Right. I'll be back. Till then, keep taking deep breaths and think beautiful thoughts.'

'Will it help?' she asked dryly.

'You never can tell,' he responded, as he walked out, and he was laughing. He did, Kim had to admit, put a different perspective on things, and she began to do all the essential tasks in preparation for lunch, which now looked as if it would be for at least three more people. How many more? she thought wryly. The children would eat with her in the kitchen, and their rooms would be ready for occupation—busily counting out knives and forks, she didn't look up as the door opened, until Luke spoke. Then she did, because his voice was taut with anger.

'We have another guest.'

'Really? Who?'

'You know damned well——' he strode over to her.

'Do I? Butch answered the bell, not me. You should have warned *him* what to say to her.'

'Then you do know?' His eyes sparked fire.

'I caught a glimpse, yes,' she admitted—'but then you arrived, so——' she shrugged and turned away. 'She should keep you busy.'

'There's enough to do, or had you forgotten that not only did I come here for peace and quiet to get on with writing a book—but I also am helping you run the bloody place?'

She hadn't forgotten, and she could see his point—but she had also had enough from him. The feelings of shame and humiliation were still there after his behaviour. Not at any cost must he know. She lifted her chin defiantly. 'I'll manage,' she retorted. 'Never think that I won't.'

'Because Butch and Theodora have mucked in? Sure. It's a novelty for them—something new.'

'It's not like that at all,' she retorted hotly. 'They're both——'

'I know what Butch is,' he cut in, 'thanks.'

'You don't at all!' she snapped. 'Now why don't you get out, and go and entertain your Miss Henderson? I'll manage without you—and just for your information, my niece and nephew are returning today and their rooms are next to mine on the top floor, so you'll have to spend your nights in your own room—or hers!' She flounced over to the sink and began to fill it with hot water. Luke was over in a second, pulling her round to face him, face dark and hard and angry.

'I've taken enough from you,' he grated, 'one way or another.'

'You certainly have!' She tried to push him away, but in vain. The next moment his mouth came down on hers in a savage, punishing kiss—and then suddenly he was lifted away from her and Kim saw Butch, furious, holding him; she gasped and tried to move forward to stop the massacre, but seemed to be rooted to the spot, then——

Crash! It was over. Luke stood rubbing his knuckles, looking at Butch lying on the floor, then looked at Kim. 'I can't punch you,' he said, 'but that's nearly as good.' And he strode out, slamming the door after him.

Butch got to his feet groggily, and held his jaw. 'Bloody hell,' he said, with feeling.

'Oh, Butch,' groaned Kim, watched him sit down,

then rinsed a clean cloth under the cold tap. 'Here.'
She held it to his chin. 'Oh—oh!'

He winced. 'Ouch—ah—that's better.' He took the
cloth from her and put it to his chin. Then he looked
up at her. She had expected to see anger in his eyes
and was surprised to see none. She was even more
astonished when he attempted a grin, then winced
again, as it apparently hurt him. 'I didn't do so well,'
he said, fingering his jaw experimentally.

'He caught you off balance,' she answered.

'No, he didn't,' was the frank answer. 'He was just
that bit quicker.'

'You're not—not angry?' she gasped.

'At him? No. At myself—yes. That's one hell of a
punch he packs. I respect that in anyone—even him.'
He opened his mouth and closed it. 'Nothing broken.'

She collapsed onto a chair, relief flooding through
her. 'Oh, Butch, what can I say?'

'As little as possible. But you can make me a coffee.'

'Yes. Yes, of course.' She hastened to do his bid-
ding, and handed him a beaker a moment or so later.
'The water was still hot.' She watched him drink it,
and her thoughts were chaotic. Luke, the man she
loved and hated, all at the same time, had quite effort-
lessly knocked out a man who was the essence of tough-
ness, and walked out with nothing more than a grazed
knuckle, and Butch, a man she liked, was sitting there,
apparently not bearing a grudge at all, accepting what
had happened with a grace that only increased Kim's
own respect for him. She sighed.

'What a mess,' she said, more to herself than him.

'You lied to me before,' he suddenly said, and she looked at him.

'What?'

'You lied. I asked you if you loved him and you said no. But you do, don't you?'

She swallowed. 'I—I don't think I've ever stopped loving him.'

'Hmm. Well, it takes all sorts to make a world.' He gave her a wry grin. 'Good job I'm an easy-going fellow.'

'You didn't——' she had to stop to stifle the threatening laughter—'you didn't look so easy-going when you marched in.'

'I thought he was *attacking* you—and then in that split second I had time to think—I realised——'

'What did you realise?'

Butch looked at her. 'Nothing.'

'Oh, come on! Don't be mean—tell me.'

'He was kissing you.'

'Well, I knew *that*!'

'But——'

'But what?' her heart had started to beat faster, because now, suddenly, she thought she knew, and she wasn't sure if she wanted to hear him say the words.

'You weren't fighting him off,' he finished.

'I was!'

'Maybe at first, but not from where I was——' he stopped. 'Sorry—why don't you just tell me to mind my own damned business?'

Kim sighed. 'I don't know what's the matter with me.' She looked at him, eyes shining with unshed tears, and heard him groan.

'Don't cry. Please don't cry, Kim.'

She sniffed. 'I won't. At least,' she amended, 'I'll try.' She blinked at him, then smiled. 'Look, that's it now. I'm sure you're quite fed up with hearing about my problems—and getting involved. Henceforth,' she stood up, 'you will see the new Kim—calm, resolute, capable.'

'Atta girl!'

'I mean it.' And she did. It was as if she saw everything clearly for the first time. And in an odd way, Butch's words had helped her to see. 'It's going to be busy here from now on, I've been all mixed up inside —but I'm not any more. You'll see.' She nodded briskly. 'I'll write you that note, then start doing lunch.'

'Thea will be over, she said to tell you.'

'Good.' She found paper and pen and began to write. Then she described the children briefly, although it was unlikely that there would be any more travelling alone, and when Butch had gone she telephoned the hospital, leaving a message for Emma to ring her when convenient. That done, she set about preparing lunch, and was joined almost immediately by Theodora.

After the totally bewildering start to the day Kim found herself, after lunch, in a completely different frame of mind. She still wasn't fully sure how it had come about, but she accepted the change gladly. She really did feel completely calm, almost as if able to stand back and see things in their proper perspective.

And yet, somehow, it had all changed after the brief and violent scene in the kitchen.

She had not seen Luke since then. He had not appeared at lunch, nor had Gail. Theodora had told Kim they had gone out, and that she had promised Luke she would help. That was all she said, and Kim had nodded.

'Fine. The longer he stays out the better.'

Theodora had looked quizzically at her. 'Hmm, things not improving yet?'

'They're not likely to. Don't worry. I'm different now—you'll see.'

And now, as they both took a welcome ten-minute break in the kitchen when all was cleared way, and the children, safely delivered by Butch, had gone out with Fiona to play, Theodora said: 'Okay, so why the sudden change? You *are* different—but how did you manage it?'

'I couldn't begin to explain. It was as if I saw everything clearly for the first time. That on top of the kids and *her* arriving—something went "click" in my brain, and I thought—the heck with everything! And that's *it*!'

'Hmm, you explain yourself very clearly—I don't think,' Theodora laughed. 'But never mind. Whatever it is, it's worked, that's the main thing. And Luke should be well occupied with you-know-who—I feel almost sorry for him—and you can get on with running this place.'

'I appreciate all your help, but you mustn't feel obliged, you know.'

'I don't,' retorted Theodora cheerfully. 'It's a change for me. Ivan pays me my salary, don't forget, and he's happy because it means he has more time to talk to Luke if I'm here—or at least,' she corrected herself, 'he did until Gail came.' She frowned. 'I don't imagine he'll let her take up too much of Luke's time.'

'What will he do?' asked Kim.

Theodora smiled. 'My dear, you may think Ivan is like a great soft teddy bear, but he's not got where he has by letting small-time actresses come between him and his work,' she smiled.

'I didn't think he was; a teddy bear, I mean,' said Kim, grinning at the picture conjured up.

'He'll think of something, never fear. Most likely send her off for a screen test to Outer Mongolia— that'll get her out of the way.' Theodora stretched and yawned. 'It should be interesting.' She looked shrewdly at Kim. 'I've met her before. She had a small part in one of Ivan's films a couple of years back—if you sneezed, you missed her, that kind of part, but it was on location in the South of France, and she had all the airs and graces of a super-star even then. And believe me, that's something she'll never be in a million years.'

'I only saw her briefly in the hall when Butch went to see who it was,' said Kim. 'She looked very stunning.'

'Probably spent three hours making up, love. Now take you—you could look like a film star if you wanted, though if you've any sense you won't bother.'

Kim laughed. 'I wouldn't know where to start. I teach in a school in the East End of London. Could you imagine the reactions if I strolled in looking like Sophia Loren?'

'Yes, I see your point. But you've got good bone structure. If ever you fancy a few make-up tips, tell me.'

'I will. How long do you think you'll be staying here?'

'Ah.' Theodora gave a mysterious little smile. 'Yes. Well——' Kim waited. 'I'm not supposed to—hmm——'

Kim laughed. 'Look, was it an embarrassing question or something? If so, I withdraw it.'

'All right. Cross your heart you'll not say a *word* to *anyone*?'

'Cross my heart.' Kim did so solemnly.

'Ivan loves the book from what he's seen—and Luke's passed the half way mark—and in a day or so I think he'll want a word with your cousin about this place.' She put her finger to her lips. 'But when Ivan asks you, you act surprised, okay?'

'Right. Oh, Theodora——'

'Call me Thea, honey, it's easier.'

'Thea then, it'll be wonderful if he used this hotel for the location shots. With Bill being in hospital, the money will be a godsend.'

'And do you know how much they'll get?'

'No. A few hundred?'

Theodora laughed, then she told her.

Kim grabbed the table. 'You're—you're kidding!'

'I'm not, love, I'm serious. It's a lot of money, right?'

'You can say that again,' Kim gasped. 'That's *marvellous*!'

'Yes. Well—not a word. Okay?' They shook hands, laughing like a pair of schoolgirls. Then Kim crossed her fingers.

'I hope it comes off,' she said.

'It will—it's almost certain. Once Ivan makes up his mind, that's it. It's going to be an upheaval all round and it means that we might just stay on here instead of moving on in a few days as would probably have happened. We're not too bad, are we?'

'Bad? I think you're all super.' It seemed the moment to mention something Kim had decided previously. 'Er—Butch, has he—have you ever thought of him doing any acting?'

Theodora stared at her. 'Butch? *Butch!*'

'Yes.' Kim stared back equally firmly.

'You mean it, don't you?'

'Yes. And don't tell him, please—but——' she stopped, feeling rather foolish all of a sudden.

Theodora's eyes narrowed; she looked into the middle distance, and she was very still. Hardly daring to breathe, Kim sat and waited. Then——

'Hmm. You know something, Kim? You've given me an idea. You really have! What made you ask?'

'Just something in his expression when I asked if he'd ever tried. Do you think——'

'I'm not sure, but don't rush me, let me think about it.' She shook her head. 'Well, well. Butch. He might be the new Rock Hudson! I must have a word with

Ivan. Not yet—but I will, I promise, when the time is right.'

'Thank you.' Kim heaved a sigh. 'I hope it works.'

'That's up to him. You might have something there. He may surprise us all—who knows. And to think we've had him under our noses all this time and never thought!' She chuckled merrily. 'I must take a good look at him when he comes in!'

At that moment, Ivan walked in. 'Ah, there you are,' he boomed. 'The worker ladies! Kim, my dear, I wonder if I might have a word with you about your cousins who own this place? I may have something to ask them.'

Kim managed to put a faintly curious but polite expression on her face. 'Of course.' She avoided Theodora's eyes, and Theodora stood and said:

'I'm off. I'll leave you to talk,' and went out. Ivan sat down heavily at the table.

'My dear, this may be a surprise to you, but this hotel would be an ideal setting for the film of Luke's book—and I would like to discuss it with them some time.' As if on cue, the telephone shrilled, and Kim picked it up. It was Emma.

# CHAPTER SEVEN

AFTER dinner Kim went up to her bedroom, utterly exhausted, and lay on the bed. The day had been a hectic one, to put it at its mildest. Her head ached, her feet ached, and her arms felt as if they might drop off at any moment. It was pleasantly cool in the room, a slight breeze ruffling the curtains, and she lay still, gradually relaxing, and thought over the events of the day from breakfast onwards.

It had been like no day in her life before, and yet now, in retrospect, she realised that she wouldn't have missed it for the world. So many things had happened—and yet so many things had been sorted out. She had help for as long as she needed it, the children were being remarkably co-operative—regarding the situation as an adventure. Ivan had organised things with Emma over the telephone. Luke had scarcely been seen. And tomorrow Butch was driving the children to hospital to see their mother and father, Theodora was organising the day's meals, and Kim was having the morning off. Butch was dropping her off in Kendal for her to have a shopping session and would collect her at lunch time; everything was fully under control.

She sighed gently, feeling her headache lifting by the minute. She resolutely refused to think about Luke; it was much easier that way. She had a book on her bedside table, but it was too much effort to pick it up. She closed her eyes for a moment; that was all she intended, but she opened them again, and it had gone dark, and she was mildly surprised to discover that she had been asleep. She switched on the light and discovered to her horror that it was past ten o'clock.

Scrambling off the bed, finding her sandals, she went to the door and ran down the stairs into the kitchen. It was empty. Fiona greeted her happily and Kim looked round. No signs of life anywhere, no crockery ready for supper, nothing. 'Where are they?' she asked the dog, bewildered. It was as though everyone had silently left —and forgotten to tell her.

Kim went into the hall, along to the reception area, then heard faint sounds from the dining room; voices, snatches of music. Puzzled, she crept along, and stopped outside the glass doors. Then she knew the reason for the silence.

A film show was in progress, and a rapt audience sat on dining chairs, the two children near the front, Miss Dines and her sister, Colonel Pickering behind them, and other, more shadowy figures ranged round the room. The film operator was Clinton, who sat half asleep, cigar at corner of mouth, on a chair behind the projector. Kim looked at the screen and recognised one of Ivan's most recent epics, a blood-and-thunder thriller that carried viewers along from first minute to last in a welter of double dealing and trickery. Kim had a faint twinge, wondering if it was suitable fare for a ten and twelve-year-old, then mentally shrugged and hoped for the best. Judging by their rapt faces, they were clearly enjoying every minute. She silently walked back to the kitchen to make herself a cup of coffee.

'Ah, that's better.' She sipped the hot coffee, savouring the peace and quiet of the empty kitchen, an unusual thing, and stroked the patient dog who had come to sit at her feet. There was a cigarette packet on the table, Theodora's, and Kim took one and lit it, feeling slightly reckless. She rarely smoked, but today was the day for unusual events, and what was one more?

She heard the back door creak, and started—then saw Fiona's tail begin to wag, and Luke walked in. For a moment he stood just inside the door looking at her. Kim didn't move, didn't speak. She merely looked back at him. She had nothing to say to him. He walked over to the stove, touched the kettle, said: 'Damn,' and spooned instant coffee into a cup. The silence stretched like a taut thread between them, and she wasn't going to break it.

Then he turned round, pulled a chair out, and sat down. Very pointedly Kim stood up, carried her cup to the sink, rinsed it, stubbed her half-finished cigarette in an ashtray and walked out of the kitchen. Outside, she took a deep breath. One to me, she thought. She went into the lounge, from where she could see the dining room door at an angle, found a magazine and began to read it.

Well, at least, thought Kim the following morning before breakfast, there can't be another day like yesterday. But that was before she bumped into Gail. . . .

It was the usual hectic breakfast rush, but she had

two assistants now, Caroline and Mark, who were delighted at the thought of serving breakfast to the five
guests. Theodora hadn't appeared, but it didn't matter,
Kim was coping very well. She looked fondly at
Caroline, dark hair in pigtails, and her brother who
stood waiting for a clean hands inspection, solemnly
took her hands, turned them over. 'Hmm, yes. Very
good.'

Caroline grinned. 'It's all right, Kim, Mum sometimes lets us help, when we're on holiday. Mark's a
dirty beast usually.'

'I'm not!' exclaimed her brother indignantly.

'But at least he washes his hands when we're serving
food. I wouldn't advise you to examine his neck,
though.'

'You cheeky thing, I——'

'All right, that's enough,' cut in Kim. 'No fighting.
It's nearly ready. Now you serve the two ladies first,
then the Colonel, then Mr Savage and Miss Henderson.'

'She's *pretty*,' sighed Mark.

'Soppy twit,' muttered his sister.

'Huh—what about you with *him*?'

'Pig!'

Kim deftly separated them, and glared at them both.
'Any more and I won't let you help. *And* I'll tell your
mum, so watch it!'

It had the desired effect, and everything went
smoothly. Kim wondered who 'him' was. Butch? Or
Luke? She had no intention of asking. And it was after
breakfast, as Kim went into the dining room to clear

the plates, that the incident happened.

The room was empty. Kim piled up some of the plates and walked towards the door. Gail stood there, looking breathtaking in a trim blue velvet trouser suit, her hair a glorious tumble of casual simplicity that didn't deceive Kim for a moment. She could almost see the lacquer holding it in place.

'I want a word,' said Gail in her husky voice.

'Yes?' Kim balanced the plates more comfortably and waited.

'Was it you who answered the telephone when I called?'

Kim knew she had a duty to the guests, but with this one she was prepared to make an exception. 'Quite possibly,' she answered, with a cool little smile. 'We get a lot of calls—I don't remember particular ones.'

'I asked if Luke was here and you tried to fob me off with some ridiculous——'

'Oh! *That* one! Was that you?' Kim laughed. 'Good gracious, didn't he tell you why? He didn't want you here.' She looked Gail up and down. 'It didn't stop you, though, did it?' She walked forward. 'Excuse me, I've work to do.'

For a split second the mask slipped and Kim saw naked spite on the beautiful face. She also saw what Gail couldn't, that Theodora had walked up quietly behind, and was waiting to come in the dining room.

'You impudent little bitch,' Gail whispered, her eyes blazing. 'You'll be sorry——'

Theodora's voice cut in. In clear bell-like tones, she said: 'Hi, Kim, I've come to help with the plates——'

then as Gail, shaking with temper, whirled round, 'Oh,
it's *you*! You're the actress, aren't you? Jean——'

'Gail!'

'Sorry, Gail—Hudson?'

'Henderson,' hissed Gail.

'That's it.' Theodora gave a throaty laugh. 'You look
so much like——' her voice tailed away, and she gave a
little smile. 'Never mind. Were you looking for Luke?
He's gone to write—doesn't want to be disturbed.
Kim, my love, Ivan said to tell you the Rolls is ready
when you are, so I'll do the washing up with the kids
and you can get off.' She smiled very charmingly at
Gail, whose expression showed a certain confusion. 'So
if you'll excuse us— that is if you've finished your little
chat with Kim?'

It seemed as if in some way, thought the amused
Kim, Gail was wondering if she had made a boob on a
magnificent scale. 'Actually, Thea,' said Kim, em-
phasising the last word, 'I don't think we had. What
were you saying, Miss Huds—Henderson? Just after
you'd called me an impudent little bitch, that is. That
I'll be sorry? How, pray? Do tell me.'

'I may have been mistaken.' It was clearly an effort.

'I think you were,' allowed Kim gently. 'Excuse me,'
and she sailed past. Gail was left standing in the doorway.

In the kitchen, Theodora collapsed at the table,
laughing, the tears streaming down her face. 'Did—did
you see——' she gasped.

'Children,' said Kim firmly, 'go and clear the tables,'
and she too sat down, shaking. The puzzled children

looked at each other and went out.

'Her face!' snorted Theodora. 'Espec—especially when I said about Ivan's Rolls? It was a *picture*.' She sobered up. 'Right, that *does* it! She clearly thought you were some poor skivvy, only fit for answering phones and clearing plates. The bitch! I hate people like her who think they can bully.'

'Thea,' said Kim, 'let's be fair. The two of us rather squashed her.'

'Oh, but we haven't finished,' said Theodora. She pulled a notebook from her bag and began to write furiously.

'What—what are you doing?'

'You'll see. You're going shopping, right? I'm just writing down a few items of make-up—you can get them from Boots.'

'But I don't——' began Kim faintly.

'Shut up, love. Don't interrupt. They won't cost you a fortune, I promise.'

'It's not that, I——'

'And then this evening I'll make you up. I shall enjoy that. And I'll make you a bet. You'll knock everyone's eyes out, and I shall watch her face!'

'But——' Kim began.

'Do hush.' Theodora tore out the paper and handed it to Kim. 'There, that's it. And there'll be a party in the lounge tonight, I'll see to that.' She smiled and stretched her arms. 'Ah, that'll be fun.'

Kim read the list. 'Hmm,' she commented.

'Right, off you go. I'll clean up here. Go on—shoo!' Theodora flapped her arms and Kim stood up.

'You're a bully too,' she said, smiling.

'I know. And I can out-bitch that Gail Henderson any time. She'll wish she'd never come.' The children came in, carrying the rest of the plates, and she too stood up. 'I'll see you later, Kim. Have fun.'

'I'll try.'

The Rolls-Royce was waiting at the front entrance, and Kim wondered, as she got in beside Butch, if Gail was watching from a window. Not that it mattered. She found to her surprise that she felt almost sorry for the actress.

The Ellisons arrived after lunch, a quiet, inoffensive middle-aged couple who came regularly for a week every year. Kim had a twinge of conscience and decided to break it to them gently that the hotel might be a shade noisier than usual owing to the fact that a film producer and friends were occupying the garden cottage. She managed it tactfully as they signed the register, and walked upstairs with them to their room. Mrs Ellison's eyes lit up when Kim had finished.

'Oh my, Jim,' she said. 'Oh *my*! Real film people!'

Mr Ellison's face registered faint dismay. 'Now, Mary,' he chided, 'don't get excited. We'll not see much of them at all.' To Kim: 'Er—they don't have *parties*, do they? Only we once had some members of a repertory company lodging next door.' Kim's heart sank. He made it sound faintly improper.

'Look—er—I can give you another room,' she began, mentally reviewing which room would be furthest from both lounge and cottage.

'Nonsense!' said Mrs Ellison crisply. 'We've always had this room, and we like it. Don't be stuffy, Jim, once you've had your sleeping pill you're away——' she turned to Kim, gentle eyes gleaming. 'I don't mind if they have parties at all.' Kim didn't tell her that they'd probably be invited too. Ivan's sense of hospitality knew no bounds. He would have invited everyone within a range of thirty miles if there had been room. She muttered something vaguely soothing and fled.

She had not seen Luke since the previous night, when she had walked out on him. And life was easier for that. But now there was vacuuming to be done, and his room was included. The children had gone with Butch to see their parents, Clinton and Theodora had vanished, Zara and Ivan were sunbathing outside the cottage—Zara indeed spent most of her days soaking up the sun—the schoolteacher sisters had gone out in Colonel Pickering's ancient Bentley for a ride, and all was quiet. Kim had no idea where Gail and Luke were and told herself she didn't care. She was, however, going to knock firmly on both their doors before going in to clean.

Gail's room was empty—at least of her. Every available surface was scattered with clothes, make-up, perfume, and it looked a mess. Kim made the bed, vacuumed, dusted, and left. And then, eventually, she came to Luke's room. There was silence from within. She knocked loudly and firmly and waited. Nothing. She opened the door with the master key and went in, pushing the vacuum cleaner with her. Luke was sitting at his desk by the window. He looked round.

'You didn't answer,' said Kim. 'I came to——'

'I can see what you came to do. I didn't answer because I didn't know who it was.' He hadn't been typing, for she had heard no noise. He had apparently just been sitting there. And he looked as if sitting there was all he was capable of doing at that moment. She had an instinctive pang of sympathy, which she immediately suppressed.

'I'll come back later,' she said, and started to back out.

'No, do it now.'

'Are you sure——' she began, politely enough.

'Sure? Of course I'm sure, damn it!' he glared at her, and Kim felt the last vestige of sympathy vanish in the face of the sudden attack.

She plugged in the vacuum, biting back a retort. She would not, ever again, argue with him. That she had decided. He moved to the window and stood watching her, his face hard and expressionless. Perhaps Gail had told him her version of the little scene in the dining room. She would imagine how it would have gone. She ran the cleaner over the carpet, back and forth, back and forth in an easy rhythm, the machine whirring gently away, until—crrrunch——! It spluttered, and Kim switched off hastily. The machine protested noisily as it coughed into silence, and she knelt down.

'Let me do it,' said Luke.

'I can manage, thank you,' she retorted. 'It's probably picked up a nail.'

He came over and knelt down, and turned the upright cleaner over. 'Unplug it,' he said.

Seething, Kim did so, and he probed gently into the bottom and pulled out a bent paper clip. 'Perhaps,' she said sharply, 'you'll be good enough in future to pick up your bits of rubbish.'

He straightened up and flung the offending clip into the waste bin. 'Leave it now,' he said. 'It looks all right to me.'

'But I——'

'I said leave it.' She sensed the hair-trigger quality of his temper, saw the tautness in his face, and a great sense of calm came over her.

Faintly smiling, she said: 'Very well. You are a guest, after all. And thank you for all your help. I take it you've finished that now?' It was said gently, pleasantly.

'You seem to have enough other assistants,' he shot back. 'I've better things to do.'

'I'm sure you have.' She looked at his empty desk and smiled. 'Ivan will be pleased you're so busy writing.'

'Get *out*.' His lips barely moved.

'I'm going. I have no desire to stay here with you a moment longer than necessary. After all, Miss Henderson might return at any time, mightn't she?' She began to walk towards the door. 'So you'd better lock your door. I won't use the master key again.'

He was in front of her, slamming the door shut, standing with his back to it, and she saw what was in his face, and her idiot calm vanished. She knew instead a great fear.

'You bitch! I——'

'I've already been called one this morning—by your
girl-friend,' she retorted. 'With your command of
words I would have thought you could think of——'

'Gail? Why?' His face was grim.

'At least you know who I'm speaking about. Why
don't you ask her?' The fear had gone. She wanted to
hurt him, to see him suffer as he had made her suffer.
'She'll tell you—if she hasn't already done so. She
called me a bitch, and told me I'd be sorry, because
I'd tried to get rid of her on the phone. Apparently she
didn't like that. And she thought I was just the maid
of all work round here, so she really let fly. People like
her do, you know. They're natural bullies—like you
are. You should be very happy together!' and so saying,
she moved forward and tried to grasp the door handle.
'Let me pass.'

He caught her arm, and Kim flailed out at him,
catching his face with her hand. The next minute she
was held, and helpless, and Luke was looking down at
her like a man who has reached the end of his tether.
His breathing was harsh, his face tormented to see, and
she gasped in pain and fear. 'Let me go!'

'When I've finished with you.'

She kicked out at him wildly, heard his shout of pain,
freed her arms and began to pummel him with her fists,
sobbing, all sense and fear gone in the need to hurt
him. A wild excitement filled her and she hit him again,
hard, across his face, then spun from him. He followed,
and she had her chance. She darted to the door, but he
was that bit faster, and caught and imprisoned her
before she could open it again. Savagely he kissed her,

bruising her mouth with his lips, holding her so tightly she feared he would suffocate her—and then——

'Luke—what the hell——!' It was accompanied by a furious rapping on the door. The voice was Gail's. As if in a sudden mutual pact, they both were still, only Luke remained holding her, and Kim felt his heartbeats and his hard body next to hers, then the storm was over, her rage spent, and in some strange way she was content to stay where she was without struggling.

The rapping rose to a crescendo. Gail's voice was hoarse with temper. 'I know you're in there. Luke, answer me. Luke!'

He seemed unaware that his hand caressed her back. Perhaps he was. And Kim felt a stirring of an excitement of a different kind within her. She had only to move, to make a sound—but she didn't.

'Luke—please——' the handle was rattled now, almost as if in entreaty. Luke moved nearer, so that their bodies were together, and Kim knew that this treacherous sensation that filled her was shared by him too. They heard muttered swearwords from the other side of the door, and Luke bent to kiss Kim again, but not savagely, only with a kind of primitive excitement and a seeking that told him his answer. And as the footsteps moved away from the door, he carried her over to the bed.

Half an hour later, when she came out of his room, she saw that Gail's door was ajar. Kim's senses were blurred with what had happened. She was scarcely aware of the face that appeared in the doorway, was indifferent to the expression on Gail's face. It wasn't until she was in the kitchen that she realised that Gail must have been sitting on the chair in her room waiting for his door to open. Kim sat down very shakily, and began to laugh. Then, suddenly, the laughter changed to tears and she put her face in her hands and wept. She wept for herself, for her own treacherous weakness, and she hated herself.

It was Theodora who found her, took one look at her, said: 'My God, Kim, what's happened?' and pulled up a chair. Kim couldn't tell her. She couldn't tell anybody. She shook her head.

'We—Luke and I—had a—a fight,' she said. It was true enough, in a way. His lovemaking had been anything but gentle.

'The beast! Let me get you a drink.'

'Coffee?'

'No, idiot, something stronger. Here.' Theodora passed Kim a glass half full of whisky. 'Drink that.'

'I—can't—I've got to get dinner ready soon.'

'No, you haven't. Ivan's orders. He wants to try his skill, and I'm helping him—and God help us all.' Kim looked up, aghast, and Theodora laughed. 'It's all right. He's damned good, actually. He's going to do a special —don't ask me what—I just slice the onions and pass him the spices and so on. Go and wash your face and he might let you watch. Zara's going to assist as well. Then we're having a party.'

Kim swallowed some of the whisky. 'I don't want to go,' she said wretchedly.

'Oh yes, you do. Did you get that make-up I listed?'

'Yes, but——'

'Good. Off you go, then. Butch'll be bringing the kids back soon. Go *on*!'

Kim finished the drink and stood up. The room swayed gracefully round, then settled. 'All right, bossy,' she answered, 'I'm going. Oh! I just remembered. I left the vacuum in——' she stopped.

'Where?'

'In Luke's room,' Kim answered in a whisper.

'My God!' Theodora looked at her very shrewdly. 'I *see*.'

'I don't—don't think you do.' Kim was near to tears again.

Theodora tried vainly to suppress a smile. 'My dear,' she said softly, 'your face gives away more than you think.'

Kim covered her burning cheeks with her hands. 'Oh,' she moaned. 'Oh *dear*——'

'Oh dear, indeed! You might well blush.'

'And Gail saw me——' she stopped. She didn't know why she had said that.

Theodora burst out laughing. 'When? Leaving his room? That's priceless!' she wiped a tear away.

'It's not funny!'

'Yes, it is! Can you imagine what's going on in *her* tiny little mind at this moment?'

Kim could. She didn't want to, but she could very easily. She closed her eyes. 'I don't feel very well.'

'Nonsense! Of course you do. In fact you look positively blooming—and I can't say I'm surprised! And you're going to the party tonight if Butch and I have to

drag you there.' Theodora poured herself a tot of
whisky. 'I wouldn't miss it for the world.'

Clinton drifted in, camera slung round his neck, and
beamed at Kim. 'Hello, ducky,' he said. 'Want your
photo taken?'

'Tonight, Clinton dear, tonight,' Theodora answered.
She passed him a glass of whisky. 'Here, get that down
you. Ivan's going to make dinner for everyone.'

'My God!' Clinton sat down and drank it in one
swallow. 'This I must see.'

Kim crept quietly out, leaving them talking, and
went to her room. As she passed the first floor she heard
raised voices from Luke's room, and went on quickly.
Gail was his problem, not hers. She had enough to
think about without worrying about a spoilt would-be
actress. And if she didn't go to the party, it would be
taken that she was scared to meet Gail. She washed
her face, put on a smear of lipstick and went down
again to the kitchen, to see Ivan already there, wearing
an absurdly tall chef's hat that Clinton had made from
paper, and butcher's apron. He was already giving his
orders, and Kim sat in a corner, well out of everyone's
way, and prepared to watch the comedy.

And comedy it was, though not without its high
points of drama as Ivan, acting the part of chef with
consummate skill, and clearly enjoying himself, made
everyone work like beavers. Theodora, crying happily,
sat and chopped several pounds of onions, Zara kept
Ivan's glass replenished with red wine, in between
adding it to the mixture in a huge pan, and Clinton kept
vanishing on mysterious errands to the cottage as some

other ingredient was remembered. Kim, classed as a visitor, was left strictly alone, except for the glass of wine that Zara brought her at one point.

'For you, my dear,' whispered Zara dramatically. 'Is he not *wonderful*? So fierce—so clevair!' Kim agreed that indeed he was, and wondered what Zara thought of Gail. She probably hadn't even noticed her.

Butch was watching television in the lounge with the children. Kim was despatched there to tell them to go and get ready for dinner, and found the Ellisons in there as well. She had forgotten all about them. She wondered, with a sudden twinge of guilt, where they had been all afternoon. Fortunately, their room was nowhere near Luke's.

'Dinner will be ready in fifteen minutes,' she announced brightly. 'Children, go and get washed.' She looked at the quiet couple, debated whether or not to warn them what to expect in the way of food, then, cowardlike, fled. They would like it. They would have to. She wasn't so sure herself, but there wasn't much she could do about it. Muttering a little prayer, she went into the kitchen again.

But she needn't have worried. Ivan had rearranged the dining room so that all the tables went to form one long table. He sat at the head of it and entertained them all while they ate, and the entire meal was a huge success. Gail, Kim noticed, was sitting next to Butch, and Luke was by Ivan, and Gail never once looked in his direction. Or in mine, for that matter, she thought. I wonder why? The wine had had its effect, and she felt pleasantly warm and reasonably happy, and if there was a party later, she would go. She might not stay late, but she would show her face, and smile coolly at Gail, and possibly ignore Luke completely; she hadn't decided.

At eight-thirty she was in her room with Theodora, and the cosmetics she had bought were spread out on the dressing table before her.

'Right,' said Theodora. 'Put that towel round your hair. Cover it all, that's it, I'll do something with that later.' She stood back, as if weighing up, making a frame of her fingers so that she appeared to be looking at Kim through a camera view-finder. 'Hmm.'

'That sounds ominous.'

'Ssh! Don't interrupt when I'm thinking. I'm just debating whether to have you looking a demure English rose or a sophisticated *femme fatale*.'

'Do I have a choice?' Kim giggled.

'You won't have in a moment if you don't shut up. Mmm, yes—the demure look, I think. That should be interesting.'

'Interesting?' Kim murmured.

'Well, comparisons are odious, love, we all know, but when you get next to Gail, who, if you hadn't noticed, plasters the make-up on with a *trowel*, you're going to make her look extremely *old*.' She said it with relish.

'How old is she?' asked Kim.

'About twenty-six.'

'Good grief!'

'Precisely. What dress are you wearing? That white one?'

'Yes. I don't have anything else.'

'That is *perfect*.' Theodora rubbed her hands together as if in anticipation. 'Oh, I'm looking forward to this. I used to be a make-up artist at Universal, you know. It'll be like old times. Now sit down, and off we go.'

Kim sat and looked in the mirror, and watched Theodora get to work. It was as impressive as seeing a painter in action, Theodora's gentle fingers smoothing, shading, pencilling the eyebrows with featherlike strokes, showing Kim how to put her own roll-on mascara on, applying the merest whisper of blusher to accentuate Kim's cheekbones, and talking all the while, telling her the beauty secrets of the stars....

The time passed swiftly. Kim put on her dress, then Theodora produced her own black holdall, said: 'Okay, kid, I'm going to do things to your hair that'll make Miss G.H.'s look like she's been dragged through a hedge.'

Kim still couldn't get over her face. She stared at herself as Theodora began brushing her hair, and said: 'I feel wonderful!'

'You look wonderful, kiddo. Just remember what I did. You've got the right face to work on, good bones— all it needs is a little touch here and there, and bingo!'

She swept Kim's hair back and curled the ends up with a heated curling wand, did miraculous things at the sides so that soft curls framed Kim's face, sprayed it with something that left her hair glossy and shiny, then pronounced the job done.

'Now go and sit on the bed and *don't move*. I'm going to have a quick make-up session myself, so you can watch me and pick up a few more tips—then we'll go down, okay?'

Bemused, Kim nodded and sat obediently on the bed, very still. Fifteen minutes later they were on their way down to the party.

# CHAPTER EIGHT

KIM suspected that Theodora had timed it so that they would be late, and her suspicions were confirmed as they neared the lounge, for the babble of noise told that the room was full. Theodora flung open the door, paused on the threshold, said: 'Hi, everybody,' and pushed Kim forward.

The hubbub ceased. All eyes turned. Kim saw, in that brief glimpse of the sea of faces, Ivan with Luke, Gail with Butch, and the rest of the crowd jumbled together. But it was Luke's face she saw the clearest of all. She saw his eyes upon her, saw what was in those eyes—then she looked away, and the spell was broken.

The talking began again, and Butch left Gail and came over to her. 'You are *beautiful*,' he said.

'Thank you, kind sir.' She bobbed a curtsey. She caught a glimpse of Gail's face as she turned to speak to Colonel Pickering who had been hovering hopefully, and shivered. 'Hadn't you better——' she nodded towards Gail, who had her back to them.

Butch grinned. 'No. Have a drink?' He guided her over to the groaning table in the far corner of the room, and Kim smiled and said hello to the bemused Ellisons who were sitting with the children, and smiled at Miss Dines and her sister who were clutching drinks as if their lives depended on it, and talking to Zara who stood tall and regal in a splendid red kaftan, and who managed to look interested in what they were saying.

Kim giggled as they reached the corner. 'Miss Dines doesn't like me very much,' she said. 'Did you see the look she gave me?'

'Yes.' Butch handed her a glass of white wine. 'You little hussy. You know why, don't you?'

'Because she fancies you? How did you get on with moving her wardrobe, by the way? I forgot to ask.'

'Then don't.' He looked at her severely. 'I barely escaped with my life, I can tell you.' He glanced across at the gallant Colonel, who was clearly delighted with Gail's attention. 'I'll tell you someone else who doesn't like you very much.'

'Gail?'

'Yes.'

'I already know,' Kim shrugged.

'Watch her, Kim, she's dangerous.'

Kim pulled a face. 'She doesn't frighten me.' She told him about the scene that morning, and he whistled softly.

'Mmm, that wouldn't exactly endear you to her, Well, stick with me, love, I'll look after you. There's dancing later. Can I book a few?'

'Of course. I'm not staying late.'

'Oh no?'

'No, honestly. I'm tired. And anyway, the children mustn't stay up too late, you know. I'll go when they go, about eleven.'

'Leaving me to the tender mercies of Gail? How could you?'

'You'll live.' She sipped her drink, then saw Ivan and Luke coming towards them.

'My dear, you look *wonderful*,' boomed Ivan. 'Doesn't she look simply superb, Luke?'

'Indeed yes.' Luke managed a thin smile. He looked, thought Kim, as though he wished he were anywhere else but there. Music began faintly from another corner of the lounge as Clinton switched on the record player.

'Ah—the music. Good.' Ivan clutched Luke's arm. 'Have a dance with Kim while I talk to Butch for a minute,' he ordered, sublimely unaware of any tension in the air. 'Now, Butch my dear chap, I've been having a few thoughts about you——' they moved away, Ivan with his arm draped across Butch's shoulder, and Luke looked at Kim.

'Do you want to dance?' he asked grimly, as if the words hurt.

'Not with you I don't,' she said, and walked away. She crossed over to where Clinton and Theodora were selecting records, and put her drink down. 'Can I have a look through?' she asked.

'Sure,' Clinton waved his hand airily. 'Come on, Thea, let's show 'em a bit of real dancing,' and they whirled away. Kim was left alone. She looked through the long-playing records idly, then stopped, looked, picked one out, and her heart beat faster. The record was one of Edith Piaf's. She was Luke's favourite singer, and during the brief period of their marriage there had been one record that they had played repeatedly, one that had said all, a beautifully tender, sad song called: '*Hymne à l'amour*' and it had at one

part, the words that they had known were intended for
them alone——'When at last our life on earth is
through, I shall spend eternity with you——' She
wanted to play the record, and she wanted to see his
face when it was played. She put it to one side—for
later. It could wait. It would be, when the time came, a
sweet revenge. For she would ensure that the record
went on just before she left the party. And perhaps he
might remember what had once been. That the record
might have an effect on her also, Kim failed to consider. But the next moment, as Butch claimed her for
a dance, she put it out of her mind.

He whirled her into the centre of the floor. 'You're
more than a hussy,' he said, 'you're a witch.'

She looked blankly at him. 'I haven't a clue what
you're talking about,' she said. It was true.

'Ivan has just suggested—as if it's been in his mind
for *years*—that I take a film test.'

She began to laugh. 'Oh, Butch—marvellous!'

'And you wouldn't have anything to do with it,
would you?' he whispered fiercely as he whirled her
round.

'Who—me? Whatever gave you——' but her face
gave her away.

He whirled her into a corner and kissed her. 'Thanks
anyway.' Then he pulled her to the drinks table. 'Let's
celebrate.'

'If I write you a fan letter when you're famous, will
you send me a signed photo?' she enquired innocently.

'I'll send you myself in a parcel. You have only to
say the word!'

The party was proceeding on its merry way. The
drink had flowed sufficiently freely for everyone to be
fully relaxed. Mr Ellison's glasses had slipped, and he
was doing a creditable tango with Caroline, while his
wife danced with Ivan, and Clinton with Mrs Beaumont. The formidable Miss Dines giggled girlishly at
something said to her by Ivan in passing, and Luke
spoke to Theodora in front of the record player. He
didn't seem to be drinking anything. Colonel Pickering
had Gail trapped in a corner and was regaling her—
judging from what they overheard as they danced past
—with his war experiences. A good time, it seemed,
was being had by everybody—or almost.

Kim and Theodora went out at half past ten to take
in the prepared sandwiches, and while they were in the
kitchen Kim told Theodora about the record she wanted
putting on. They went back in, and all was arranged.

At ten to eleven Kim nodded to Theodora and
started to dance with Butch. As she passed the two
children, she whispered: 'Ten minutes more, okay?'
They pulled faces, but nodded. She went over to the
corner and said: 'Can I have a drink?'

'Sure. What?'

'Gin and tonic, please.'

Butch poured out and handed her one. 'Cheers.'

'Cheers.' She could see Luke. Gail had escaped from
the Colonel and was talking to him, her back to them.
It was an eloquent back. Gail was not having the best
time in the world. And Kim could see Luke's face
clearly. He looked like a man who was bored with the
world.

Then the music swelled, and Kim felt the old familiar shiver run down her spine. Butch whispered: 'What is it?'

'Ssh—just a minute. I'll tell you——' she stopped. Edith Piaf's voice came, and suddenly, very suddenly, Kim wished she had not done what she had, but it was too late. 'If the sun should tumble from the sky, if the seas should suddenly run dry, if you loved me, really loved me, let it happen, I won't mind——'

And Luke looked across the room at her, across the years in between, and time stood still. It was as though everyone else in the room faded into nothing—as though—Kim couldn't breathe. The room was blurred, misty, unreal. Only Luke's face was clear, and she knew she would never forget what she saw in his eyes. Then he turned, put his glass down, and walked out of the room.

Kim took a deep, shuddering breath. Butch asked, very quietly: 'What was all that about?'

She looked at him. 'The song—it meant something to us once.' She closed her eyes. 'I wanted to see——' she stopped.

'And I think you did, didn't you?'

'I should never have done it.'

'No, perhaps you shouldn't.' He smiled slowly. 'The man's a fool.'

'Why?' she could scarcely mouth the word.

'Because you love him.'

'I think I'd better take the children to bed——' she faltered.

'Yes, a good idea.' He sighed. 'Oh, Kim, what a

funny world we live in.'

'I hope you make it with the screen test.' She
squeezed his hand. 'Thanks for looking after me.'

'I'm going to make Miss Dines' evening for her—
watch me.' He gave her a little salute and walked off.
Kim saw him foxtrotting off with a delighted Miss
Dines as she went over to collect the reluctant children.
They said goodnight to everyone and left.

Upstairs all was quiet. Kim persuaded Caroline and
Mark to have a good wash, told them she would be up
to bed after she had let Fiona out, and went down. The
back door was closed, but Fiona was nowhere to be
seen. Kim called her, then went to the door and opened
it. It was unlocked. She called Fiona, and the dog came
up woofing and wagging her tail. Then, in the trees, she
saw a shadowy figure, and knew it was Luke. She didn't
want to see him, she didn't want to speak to him. She
patted the dog and walked quickly out and ran up to
her room as if pursued.

The music thundered out from the lounge, fading as
she reached the upper floor, and she walked along
slowly, went in and tucked the children up, and into
her room. The party was over. The sweet revenge she
had planned had recoiled on her. She had seen Luke's
face, and she had known her own reaction, and nothing
would ever be the same again. As soon as the Barnes'
were back, she would leave. She would see Emma, and
tell her, as briefly as possible, why, then she would go.
The Barnes' would manage, with the children's help,
and possibly that of Theodora, because it looked as
though they would be a while, and Kim would be free

to get away, and to forget.

She stood by the open window, seeing the stars in the dark night sky, hearing the faint music, and her heart was heavy. It had all gone so wrong, so very wrong. How amusing it had seemed, to dress up to make Gail feel humiliated. And what did it matter? She was welcome to him, thought Kim. They were two of a kind. She turned away from the window and went and lay on the bed, in her dress, and there she fell asleep.

When she woke the first pale streaks of sunlight were colouring the sky. She was cold, and her pillow was damp with the tears she thought she had dreamed. Stiffly she rose, took off the dress and got into the bed. Another day had nearly begun, and what would this one hold? Only time would tell.

When she awoke again it was seven-thirty. She wondered, as she washed in the bathroom, what time the party had finished. There might be no one for breakfast. The thought was almost funny, and Kim visualised herself and Fiona sharing bacon and eggs for seven.

She went downstairs in pyjamas and dressing gown, and there were no sounds from anywhere. She looked into the dining room and saw that the table was still in one. She mentally shrugged. Let them all continue eating like that for breakfast. It didn't matter.

'Hello, Fiona, come on out, old girl.' She unlocked the back door and made the first welcome cup of coffee of the day, standing at the door to drink it. There seemed no point in starting breakfast for another hour, and perhaps not even then. She would go and have a leisurely bath and then decide. It was all too much trouble at the moment to think. She felt ill. There was a leaden feeling to her limbs, and a swimming sensation in her head. What did I drink? she thought. Not much, a couple of gins, some wine, that was all. She put her hand to her forehead, and it was burning. Unsteadily she walked to the table and put the cup down. If she left the door open, Fiona would come in when she was ready—she never went far. It seemed important to get back into bed, and to tell someone—but whom? She could hardly wake anyone. The sensation was growing worse. The room spun round, and she could hardly stand. Kim was frightened. Staggering slightly, she made her way to the door, then slowly, laboriously, along the hall, and up the stairs.

She had to hold on to the banister, and every step took an age. Then the last stage of the journey, and she reached Caroline's door, and opened it.

'Caroline?'

The girl stirred, then sat up sleepily. 'Yes?'

'It's me—Kim—I don't feel very well. I'm going back to bed. When you get up, would you tell Theodora or someone?'

'Kim?' Caroline jumped out of bed and went over to her. 'What's the matter? Shall I get someone now?' Her eyes were wide and frightened.

'No, let them sleep. I just need to lie down and rest. Later will do. I think the party went on late—they won't wake yet——' her voice tailed away. She didn't want to alarm her young cousin. 'Go back to bed for half an hour.'

'I'll get up now, Kim. Honest, I'm wide awake. Get into bed and I'll see you tucked in.' For a twelve-year-old, thought Kim, as they went into her room, Caroline was very composed. She made her get in, pulled up the sheet and coverlet and stood looking down at her. 'Just lie there. I'll not be long.' And she went out.

Time drifted past in a waking dream. Then the door opened and someone walked in. It wasn't until he reached the bed that Kim realised it was Luke.

She stared at him through a mist of incomprehension. 'I don't want you,' she murmured.

'Caroline tells me you're ill.'

'Go away.'

He put his hand to her forehead. 'I'm going to get a doctor.' She couldn't argue because she had no strength. She looked at him helplessly, and tears filled her eyes. 'Have you looked in a mirror?' he said gently, and sat on the bed.

It seemed such an absurd question that she didn't bother to answer.

'Because you're covered in spots.'

'Don't be silly——' she put her hand to her neck. It itched.

'Just lie still, Kim. Is there anything you need? A drink, maybe?'

'No. Fiona's out——'

'I got her in. Caroline's getting Theodora over here as soon as she sees signs of life in the cottage. I'll phone the doctor now and tell him what's wrong.' He stood up. 'You'd better try and recall what childhood diseases you've had, because it looks remarkably like chickenpox to me,' and with that he went out quietly, closing the door after him.

Through the fog of her mind, Kim tried to think. Chickenpox—and young Johnny Gibson had started with that three weeks ago. And I've never had it, she thought, but of course I imagined I was immune.... She closed her eyes. I hope Caroline and Mark have had it, she thought. Oh dear.... But it was rather a lot of trouble to think clearly, so she gave up the attempt.

Luke returned after a while. 'The doctor will come in later,' he said. 'I've brought you a cup of tea and some toast. Can you sit up?'

'Yes.' She found the strength, and pushed herself up. 'Thank you.'

'No one is awake yet. I believe the party went on until four a.m.,' he said.

'Weren't you there?'

'No. But I heard it. So a late breakfast won't come amiss—if anyone wants one at all. And you've lost one guest.'

It sank in slowly as she sipped the welcome cup of tea. She frowned.

'Who?'

'Gail Henderson.'

'Oh.'

'She had an urgent call to go back to London for an audition.'

There didn't seem anything to say to that, so Kim didn't bother. Something else was bothering her. If Luke had heard the party going on so late, he must have been awake himself. And he hadn't returned to the party. And he had left when the Edith Piaf record was being played.

'I'm sorry,' she said.

He looked faintly surprised. 'About Gail?'

But she hadn't meant that. She wasn't sure what she had meant. She shook her head. 'It doesn't matter. You don't have to stay. You don't want to catch anything, do you?'

'I've already had chickenpox. Eat your toast.'

'I'm not hungry.'

'Then I'll have it.' Luke crunched his way through the piece.

Kim lay back and closed her eyes. 'Please go away.'

'All right, I will.' He picked up her empty cup, and the plate, and went out. Kim was alone. She slept for a while, was vaguely aware of the door opening and closing once or twice, but no one came in, and the time passed in a blurred haze. Then the doctor arrived. He confirmed Luke's diagnosis of chickenpox, told her to keep well away from everyone save those who had already had it for at least six days, left a prescription for lotion to be dabbed on her spots, said briskly—and slightly ominously in Kim's fevered opinion—that he was to be phoned if she got worse, and left after a cheerful good morning.

She lay back feeling very sorry for herself and Theodora said: 'Never mind, love. Ivan's looking after everything.'

'What do you mean?'

'You'll see.' Theodora winked. 'Things are getting moving now. Ivan's taken over here and you've nothing to worry about. I'm your official nurse—isn't that nice? Good job I had chickenpox when I was a kid—God, you look a mess!'

'Thanks,' muttered Kim.

'Cheer up. At least G.H. has gone—hurrah! What a coincidence, her having to go for an audition!'

'Hmm, a very odd coincidence, if you ask me. Ivan didn't make any phone calls yesterday, did he?'

'He has lots of friends in lots of theatres, my love. 'Nuff said?'

Theodora trotted out, promising to look in later with the prescription, for which Butch was being despatched post haste to Kendal, and Kim was alone again. But not for long. Caroline and Mark, another two who had had the dreaded disease, came to tidy up for her and report on the latest developments downstairs. Ivan had been busy on the telephone, they told her, Butch had gone out in the Rolls, Luke had been sent to his room and told to keep on writing until he dropped if necessary, and Theodora, Clinton and Zara were making a great deal of noise preparing lunch, and Miss Henderson had been taken by Butch earlier to catch a train to London and the Ellisons were suffering from hangovers, and Miss Dines and her sister were sitting in the lounge dozing, and Colonel Pickering was in the conservatory, presumably writing his never-ending memoirs, and everything was under control and did Kim feel better?

Kim felt exhausted after that saga, but yes, she admitted, she was feeling slightly better, and almost ready for a little light lunch.

Butch came in shortly afterwards, bearing a large bottle of flesh-coloured lotion, closely followed by Theodora. 'I've come to rub on this stuff for you,' he said cheerfully.

'Oh, no, you haven't,' retorted Theodora, grabbing the bottle from him. 'I've met your sort before.'

He laughed, and sat on the bed, peering closely at Kim. 'Yuk!' he exclaimed, 'you look a bit different from last night.'

'Everyone seems determined to make me feel good,' protested Kim. It was impossible to feel ill for long with them. She decided that she might as well stop feeling sorry for herself and enjoy being an invalid for a few days. And later she found out precisely why Ivan had taken over, and how.

He had arranged with a London agency for a cook and housekeeper to be sent up for as long as they were needed. They arrived after lunch, and Theodora came up to report to Kim. 'I shudder to think how much it's costing him,' she said, 'but at least everything will run smoothly now. They're super-efficient, and have already taken over in the kitchen. Even poor Fiona's been pushed into the lounge, the washer's going full blast, vacuum ditto, and it's action stations all round.'

And that means, thought Kim, that as soon as I'm better I can leave. She wondered why that should have a depressing effect on her; it was, after all, what she wanted. The day passed, and night came, and Theodora, seeing her feverishness, took a camp bed into Caroline's room and slept there. In the still hours of the night when all was quiet, and the world slept, Kim woke up from a dreadful dream and lay, drenched in perspiration, thinking she was going to die. She practically crawled to the bathroom, determined not to wake Theodora, and fell on her way out. It took her ten minutes before she managed to pull herself up to her feet to begin the long walk back to her room. Everything swam round, and she stood in the doorway, fighting for control, looking at her bed, so near, and yet so incredibly far away, and prayed she would reach it.

Then a pair of strong arms took hold of her and a voice said, 'Relax. You're safe,' and as she started to fall, she was picked up and carried over to the bed. Luke tucked her in and stood there, bending over her, but he seemed very distant, and she could scarcely hear what he was saying for the mists that swallowed her up, and she was hardly aware that it was him, and it hurt to think at all, and the effort of wondering how he had got there was too great, so she stopped trying.

A cool hand on her forehead, words gently soothing her; she was warm, and safe, and comfortable, and aware that he sat on a chair at the side of the bed, and so she drifted off into a deep warm sleep. A hand was holding hers, and she stirred and half woke up. The shadowy figure was still there and now it seemed like a dream again, but not a nightmare, very pleasant, and she was safe, and she wasn't going to die; she was going to get better.

When Kim woke in the morning the fever had gone and she felt as if she had slept for days and was strong enough to cope with anything. She looked at the chair beside her bed, and wondered how it had got there when it had been further away. Perhaps Theodora had come and moved it during the night for some reason best known to herself. Kim sat up, pushed her pillows into a more comfortable position behind her, and reached for a magazine.

When a bleary-eyed Theodora came in bearing a cup of tea, Kim greeted her with a cheery: 'Good morning,' and smiled through her spots.

'Ugh! You look disgustingly healthy,' grumbled Theodora, setting the cup down. '*I've* just had the most uncomfortable night on a blasted camp bed so that I could nurse the invalid if necessary and you look as though there's absolutely nothing wrong with you— except for a spotty complexion. You're a fraud!'

Kim laughed. 'Sorry, sorry. But I feel well. And I'm *starving*!'

Theodora sat down. 'Did you move the chair during the night?' Kim asked her.

'No. I'd got better things to do, ducky—like trying to get some sleep, you know, simple things like that.' She pulled a face.

'Look, you can sleep in your own bed tonight, honestly. I'm tons better.'

'I can see you are. Sorry I was grumpy.' Theodora frowned. 'Did I hear a bang in the night? I seem to remember something——'

'No, don't think so.' Kim searched her memory, and it seemed an elusive dream slipped away and was gone. 'Unless it was me moving the furniture.' She laughed at the absurd thought.

'Yes, well, I'll go and get your breakfast. Then it's

lotion time—do they itch?'

'Yes, terribly.'

'Huh—serves you right,' she grinned at Kim, and ducked the magazine that came sailing after her. 'I'll go and see if the two guardians of the kitchen will allow me to bring you food.' Off she went. Kim looked at the chair and frowned. Now what had she thought of before? No good, it was gone. She picked up another magazine and began to leaf through it.

She had a constant stream of visitors that day—at least, it seemed like it. The children, Clinton bearing flowers, Butch with a pile of paperback books he had bought in Kendal for her, Theodora several times, bearing messages from Ivan and Zara, neither of whom had ever had chickenpox and were understandably wary. Zara had sent a small bottle of perfume as a gift. Kim was touched by their consideration. The notable exception to the list of visitors was Luke. She didn't see him at all. But then she hadn't expected to. There was also a message from the hospital via Butch, who had taken the children again, to say that Bill was progressing nicely and would probably be home in two weeks on condition that he rested. Emma had also written her a letter. When she was alone, Kim opened it, and began to read: 'Dear Kim, Sorry you're laid low with chickenpox. It's a relief the children have had it. I'm only sorry you were landed with everything like that, but it all seems to be working out nicely. Butch is very sweet and told me all about how Mr Zolto has taken charge of everything, and I must say I'm looking forward to meeting him—fancy the hotel being used in a film! It's all like a dream. My main worry is Bill, of course, and if there's cameras and everything all over the place we'll just have to keep out of the way and keep quiet—but he's going on so well now they've fitted this thing, he's like a different man. The money from Mr Zolto sounds too good to be true—I'll believe it when I see it! And to think it all started with Mr Savage arriving.'

Kim put the letter down for a moment. A lot of things had happened since Luke's arrival. She began to read again. 'Must go now, love. It was lovely to see the children. I didn't realise how much I was missing them. I hope the Ellisons weren't too shocked at the crowd there. They're such a *quiet* couple——' Kim grinned at that, wishing Emma could have seen them at the party—'but I'm sure the others—especially the Colonel —are enjoying everything. See you soon, love, Emma.'

Kim put the letter away in its envelope and lay back. Everything was working out well for everybody. The hotel was running smoothly, the guests having a whale of a time, the children enjoying themselves far better than if they had stayed at their aunt's—and me, she thought, I'm only in the way. Everyone was being kind, but they weren't really there to play nursemaid. They were there to do business with Luke, and with Emma and Bill. Kim stared at the ceiling, and tears filled her eyes. Luke would have no more distractions if I left, she thought. Gail's gone. And so should I go. She wondered if her car was ready, and the slowly formulating plan began to take shape. Would Butch help? She would ask him to telephone the garage later. It was, after all, a perfectly natural query. If it was, and could be collected or delivered, then she could leave just as soon as she was strong enough to drive. And that would be soon, she knew, for she felt so much better already. She would write to Emma and explain as briefly as possible. Emma would understand.

'Are you awake?' It was Theodora, creeping in quietly. Kim jumped guiltily, as if her thoughts were written for all to see.

'Oh! Yes—of course.' She looked at her. Theodora would understand as well. She already knew so much. 'Thea, sit down, love, I've got something to tell you.' Kim patted the bedside chair.

Theodora frowned and looked very suspiciously at her. 'What have you been up to?' she said accusingly.

'Nothing—yet. But just listen to me for a minute— please.' Kim began to tell her.

# CHAPTER NINE

'No! Most definitely no! You are absolutely *mad*!'
Theodora stood up and began pacing the room. 'Good
grief, you've been ill in bed for one day, and I thought
how well you were doing, and then you come up with
this crackpot idea——'

'Thea! Please,' Kim begged. 'You don't understand——'

'You listen to *me* for a minute. You're sick. You've
got chickenpox, you idiot, not a head cold. Damn
Luke! And do you think I'm bothered about being a
nursemaid, as you call it? Heavens, it makes a nice
change from dashing about the world, living out of a
suitcase and soothing spoilt starlets when they start
getting in a temper because someone else had two more
lines than them! Now I don't want to hear any more
nonsense like that. Leaving indeed. Huh!' and she
glared at Kim, arms akimbo.

Kim shrank down into the bed and pulled the covers
up. 'Can I consider myself told off?' she whispered.

'You damned well can!' Then Theodora's face
softened. 'All right, don't sink right down or you'll
suffocate. Sit up. And we'll talk sensibly. Now,' she sat
on the edge of the bed, 'first, you couldn't go anywhere
for a few days because, however good you feel, you'd
be too weak to drive—you could have an accident or

154

anything. Second, we're the intruders, not you. You
fixed us up with that nice cottage when we arrived, and
you've been managing everything very nicely for your
cousin, so why should you think we want to get rid of
you?'

'You know it's not only that,' Kim pointed out. 'It's
*him*. I'm so unhappy——' and she burst into tears.

'I know, love, I know.' Theodora put her arms round
Kim's shaking shoulders. 'I've seen it, I know. Don't
cry, no man is worth it.'

'But I love him—and—and it's tearing me
apart——'

'I don't think he's so happy, either.' Theodora passed
Kim her handkerchief from by the pillow. 'Dry your
eyes. It happens, you know. Two people can just strike
sparks off each other—and, as you say, end up tearing
each other apart. And it must be hell for you both,
staying in the same place——' she closed her eyes. 'Let
me think for a minute. I've got to think. I'm getting an
idea, but I'm not sure what it is yet.' She stood and
went over to the window.

Kim waited, silent, watching her. Theodora's reaction to her plan had been one of absolute horror—at
first. Then, after that shock outburst, she had calmed,
and now she was thinking about something important.
But what?

Theodora turned. 'I'll have to have a word with
Ivan,' she said. 'He'll realise, when I put it to him——'

'But——'

'Ssh! I'm not saying another word till I've seen him.
Now,' she looked at her watch, 'it's nearly dinner time.

I'll talk to him after he's eaten—he's always more amenable to suggestion then—and I'll bring your dinner up straight after. Be patient. I've got to get him on his own.' And off she went. Kim opened a book and began to read it. She hadn't the faintest idea what it was about, even after reading the first page several times, but she ploughed resolutely on, willing the time to pass quickly.

It seemed to Kim that weeks passed before she heard the familiar steps in the corridor outside her room. Glancing at the clock, she saw that it was precisely fifty minutes since Theodora had left. She put the book down.

Theodora handed her the tray, then went to close the door. 'Eat up,' she said in helpful tones.

'How can I when I'm waiting——'

'If you don't eat I won't tell you.'

Kim sighed and began the rather delicious-looking roast beef. 'That's better. Right. I've seen Ivan alone and I've explained the situation to him very briefly and he's agreed.'

Kim waited. 'He has an apartment in—wait for it— a castle. And that's where we're going to stay until you're better.'

'A castle?'

'Yes. A real genuine fourteenth-century castle only about two hours' journey from here. It's on the borders of southern Ayrshire, by the sea, and he was presented with the apartment by the grateful citizenry of the place for putting them on the map. Remember his film *Flashpoint at Noon*?'

'Yes. I saw it—you mean *that* castle? The one in the film?'

'The very same. Dalmain Castle.'

'You say—*we're* going?'

'You're not fit to go alone. And I've not had a holiday for years. Yes, I'm driving you there. We'll just take off in a couple of days, stay until you're fully recovered, and then see what to do. I'm looking forward to it, quite honestly. I was there on location, but I never got to see this apartment they gave him afterwards.'

'You're very kind, Thea.'

She grinned. 'I know.'

'But what about—er—Clinton? Won't he mind?'

'My love, Clinton and I have a very good relationship. We're more like brother and sister. Or hadn't you noticed we're always fighting?' Theodora smiled. 'It'll be interesting to see if I miss him, actually.'

'Does he—Luke, I mean, need to know we're leaving?'

'Not if you don't want him to.'

'Then I'd rather just go, I think.' Kim bit her lip. 'It might be better that way.'

'Suit yourself. Anyway, Ivan will phone and ask them to warm it up or whatever it is they do in castles —probably light a few rush torches on the walls! And we'll buy food on the way, and Bob's your uncle.'

'Did Ivan wonder why——'

'Well, he had noticed something, naturally—and quite frankly, he agreed with the point I made, that Luke would probably write quicker when you'd gone.'

That seemed to sum it up exactly. Kim remembered
the time she had gone into Luke's room, and he had
been sitting at the desk, not writing, not doing anything. The sooner they got out of each other's lives,
the better. Then she remembered what had happened
afterwards, and was filled with deep shame. That too.
They would only destroy one another—she took a
deep breath. 'Thanks, Thea,' she said quietly.

Much later that night she lay awake in bed unable to
sleep. Her thoughts were confused and chaotic, she
was physically uncomfortable, and she was thirsty and
hungry. Everywhere was dark and silent as she put
on her dressing gown and went downstairs to the
kitchen.

She blinked as she switched on the lights. Everything gleamed as it had never gleamed before. She felt
almost guilty as she made herself coffee watched by
a sleepy Fiona—who looked as though she too had
been well brushed. She took three biscuits from the
tin, and crept upstairs again. She stumbled on the land-
ing and held on tight to the rail, holding her breath in
case anyone woke. Somewhere, a door creaked, but that
was all. Breathing again, she crept up and into her
room. The little expedition had tired her, and she realised the wisdom of Theodora's remarks. She would
not be fit to drive anywhere.

She ate the biscuits, then took off her nightgown
ready to smooth lotion on to her itching spots. 'Ah!' she
gave a beautifully relieved sigh as the cool balm soothed
away the irritation. It was bliss. There was obviously

something anasthetic in the lotion, for it gave her relief for several hours. She dabbed as much as she could on her arms and shoulders and heard Luke's voice from the doorway:

'Are you——' he stopped. Kim turned, snatching up her nightgown to hide her nakedness.

'I'm all right,' she gasped. 'I was just—putting on——' she stopped as he came nearer. 'Go away. I'm all right.'

'I'm not going to hurt you.' His voice was harsh. 'I heard noises and thought you'd fallen again.'

'What do you mean—again?'

'Don't you remember?'

'No.'

'You went to the bathroom last night, and fell. I brought you back here.'

It had been a dream, surely? And the holding hand —that too? She looked blankly at him. 'I dreamt it,' she said.

He shrugged. 'It doesn't matter. Turn round, I'll do your back.'

'No.' She was breathless and afraid. She knew him— but worse still, she knew herself. Knew the treacherous weakness that could overtake her.

'Don't be stupid. You can't reach.' He took the bottle and the wad of cotton wool and went behind her. Kim bit her lip to stop herself from crying out as she felt the cool caressing movement of his hand on her back. Shoulderblades, spine, waist, then round the side and under her arm, then the other side, then it wasn't the cotton wool, it was his hand rubbing her gently, and the fire began, and she heard his breathing change, and she wondered if he could hear her heart beating —then he was saying: 'There too?' And his hand was on her breast. 'Why is your heart pounding so?' he asked. 'Are you frightened?'

'Yes. Go away.' She heard the chink of the bottle, then both hands were round her body.

'It's nearly done now. Is that better?'

She couldn't breathe. The blood pounded in her head and she was drowning and she no longer cared. 'I have no spots there——' she began.

'No, I know.'

'Please leave me now——' she half turned, but she was too near the bed, and fell on to it. And it was too late.

He was gentle, gentler than he had ever been before. And when he left her, it was nearly dawn.

Kim saw the cup of coffee as she got out of bed. Cold and forgotten, it stood accusingly on the dressing table. She carried it into the bathroom and emptied it into the bowl, rinsed it away, then washed. Then she dressed herself. It took time, and it tired her, but she could manage it. When Theodora came in it was to see Kim sitting on the bed reading a magazine. She put down the tray.

'Good grief! How did you manage that?'

'Very slowly,' answered Kim. 'Can we go today— please?'

'Today? It's much too soon——'

'*Please*. If I stay here any longer I'll go mad!'

Theodora frowned. 'Have you and Luke had a row?'

Kim didn't answer. She couldn't. Theodora sat down heavily on the bed. 'Oh, my God, he's not—no, I don't want to know.' This, as Kim opened her mouth to speak. She looked at her watch, frowned as if making a decision. 'All right, so be it. But we go in my car.'

'I didn't know you'd got one!'

'A Rover, yes. We travel in convoy, love, Ivan and Zara in the Rolls, Clinton and Butch and me in the Rover. Very impressive. It's maroon as well, you see.' She grinned. 'You'd better get packed—no, I'll help you. You're not strong enough. Eat your breakfast.' She stood up. 'I'll go and fling a few clothes together and be back soon. Butch will keep an eye on the kids until your cousin comes home.' She reached the door. 'And don't worry about bumping into Luke. He came down to grab some breakfast, said he was going back up to write, and now there's a huge "Do not Disturb" sign on his door.'

Kim, alone, finished her breakfast and began to gather her clothes together, ready to pack. If she had had any doubts about the wisdom of what she was doing, they were dispelled by what happened during the night. If ever she was to lead a normal, happy life, she had to get away—as far away—from Luke as possible.

She wrote a letter to Emma and left it in Caroline's room for her to give to her mother when she saw her. Then she waited for Theodora to return.

It was Butch who came up first though. 'Thea's just told me you're leaving,' he said. 'I'm sorry, love.'

'We'll keep in touch,' answered Kim. 'I want to know how you get on with that screen test anyway. Promise you'll let me know?'

'Promise. Good or bad, I'll write you.'

She leaned over and kissed his cheek. 'Don't forget now.'

He took her hand. 'Next time,' he said, 'I won't miss him.'

'There won't be a next time.' She smiled sadly. 'That's why I'm going. I should never have played that record, should I? It hurt me far more than it hurt him.'

'I wonder,' he shrugged.

'What do you mean?'

'I saw his face too, don't forget. He looked like he wanted to die. I felt sorry for him, really sorry.'

'He'll change after today, you'll see.' There were tears in her eyes. 'And anyway, I don't know why I'm boring you with my troubles.'

'That's what friends are for. Hey, you don't have any sisters who look like you, do you?'

Kim laughed. 'No! But you make me feel good. Just wait till you're famous—you'll be fighting the girls off, then. And I'll say, "I knew him before he was a star", and no one will believe me.'

Theodora came in. 'Break it up, you two. We've got packing to do, remember?'

Butch stood up and hugged Kim, nearly breaking her ribs. 'I'll be seeing ya, kid,' he said in a gorgeous American accent. 'Look after yourself.'

When he had gone, Theodora looked at Kim, whose

expression was sad. 'Don't worry about Butch,' she said. 'He has the girls falling all over themselves to get near him when we're on location.'

'He does? Mind, I'm not surprised. He's not conceited, though, is he?'

'No, funnily enough, he's not. He'll meet a nice girl one day, and settle down, you'll see. He likes you a lot, but, as he told me, you're different.'

'I hope he meant it as a compliment!' smiled Kim.

'He did. He also knows you're dotty about your ex. Funny thing is——' Theodora stopped. 'No, never mind.'

'Don't leave it there. What?'

'Well, he said something odd to me just a day or so ago. He said—he thought Luke was crazy about you too, but didn't know it.'

'He despises me.'

'Butch doesn't think so. However,' Theodora shrugged, 'men always get it wrong, don't they? Now, where are your cases?'

Half an hour later, when at last they were ready to set off, Kim wondered if she hadn't made a big mistake in deciding to leave. She felt weak and breathless, and had to sit on the bed. She didn't want Theodora to see, or she might take one look at her and refuse to go, and that mustn't happen. Once they were on their way, it wouldn't matter. She forced herself to breathe deeply and steadily, to sit very still and conserve what little energy she possessed.

She wanted nothing more than to get back into bed, lie down, and sleep. But first, there was the journey....

'You look terrible.' Theodora's voice came from the doorway. 'Honestly, Kim, you're not fit.'

'Yes, I *am*,' whispered Kim.

'Hmm. Well, you lie down in the back and we take a blanket and you cover yourself with it—and that's an order!'

'I'll do anything you say.'

'You really are desperate, aren't you?'

'Yes.' It took all her strength to speak.

'All right. I'm as daft as you are—but come on. We're ready.'

Slowly they went down the stairs. Butch had put their cases in the Rover, which stood at the front. Kim said goodbye to the children, and Clinton, who waited in the hall, and who told her that Ivan and Zara sent their best, but thought it better to keep well out of germ range and hoped she wouldn't mind.

Butch tucked her in the back, gave her a little salute, and closed the door. Then they were off. As they went down the drive, Kim looked out of the back window. It seemed to her that a curtain stirred at the window that was Luke's. But it might have been her imagination.

They had taken a flask and some sandwiches for the journey, because, as Theodora said as they drove away, although it wasn't a long trip she had no intention of driving fast—and she certainly had no intention of stopping at a motorway service area with the possibility of Kim spreading alarm all round.

'I mean, can you imagine,' she said, her voice slightly raised over the purr of the engine, 'you walking in all covered in spots and everyone fleeing to their cars? There could be a multiple pile-up—and it would all be your fault.'

Kim smiled faintly. 'Not a pretty sight,' she agreed. 'Oh, Thea, isn't it a good job I didn't break out in them two night's ago, with all that lovely make-up on, and my hair all beautiful? I'd have caused a sensation at the party!'

'I wonder how dear Gail's going on at her audition?' mused Theodora.

'Is it a genuine one?'

'Oh yes. Ivan wouldn't do anything underhand like that. It'll be all above board—in fact, if she gets the job, good luck to her.'

'What's it for?' asked Kim.

'Some series of commercials they're doing for pipe tobacco. At least it got her out of Luke's hair for a while.'

Kim digested that piece of information in silence. She hadn't really given Gail another thought.

'Has anyone ever got the better of Ivan?' she asked.

Theodora laughed. 'If they have, I've not met them,' she admitted. 'He's a multi-millionaire, you know.'

'Good grief! And he cooked dinner for us the other night!'

'Didn't he tell you? He likes the simple life——' there was a long pause, 'occasionally.'

'Yes, he told us when he first arrived—and Luke's face was a picture when he said it. But, let's be fair,' added Kim, 'he doesn't put on airs and graces. He had everyone to those parties, and made them feel at home.'

'That's the secret of his success. He genuinely likes people. Oh, he's hard—and he can be ruthless if he wants something—but he's got a kind streak in him. Incidentally, he'd kill me if he thought I'd told anyone, because it doesn't go well with his image of the tough tycoon—but I've seen him with tears in his eyes at a kids' party at an orphanage in Barcelona. And the next day I took them a cheque for two thousand dollars. That never got into the papers, because he made sure it didn't.'

'My God!' whispered Kim.

'Yes. Precisely. You'll read about all his ex-wives in the gossip columns, and all about his latest film, and who he's been seen with at a nightclub, but you won't read about the other things he does quietly because he thinks it's a sign of weakness and people would laugh at him. If only he knew they wouldn't!'

'You think a great deal of him, don't you?'

'I've never really thought too deeply about it, but— yes, I do. More in a daughterly way than anything, I suppose, certainly nothing romantic, or I wouldn't get on so well with Zara. And I like her too, in a funny sort of way. She's a very good mimic, incidentally. You should see her do Marlene Dietrich, and Zsa-Zsa Gabor.'

'It's funny, isn't it?' said Kim. 'I'm only starting to find out about them now I've left.' She heaved a sigh. 'Never mind.'

'I'll tell you lots more when we arrive. Just shut your eyes now and rest. You're an invalid, remember?'

'Yes, aunty.'

'And don't be cheeky! Go to sleep.'

Kim did so. When she woke up they were arriving at the castle.

The apartment was beautiful. Large too, with three bedrooms, sitting room, kitchen and modern bathroom. A very welcoming fire crackled in the huge fireplace in the sitting room, and there was a vase of fresh flowers on the table. Kim looked round her in delight—and began to feel better.

'Wow!' Theodora's voice was eloquent. 'This is the life, eh?' She went over and touched the deep red velvet curtains that swept the floor. 'I could live here!'

'We're going to, for a few days anyway, aren't we?' Kim sat on the long deep settee by the fire. 'Mmm, I feel much better.'

'Considering you slept all the way here, I'm not surprised,' was Theodora's dry comment. 'I'll phone Ivan and tell him we've arrived. I'll not be a minute.' She went out into the hall of the apartment. Kim could hear her voice faintly, but no words. The call was brief, then Theodora came in again. 'Right, coffee, then lunch,' she said. 'All is running smoothly back at the ranch—so far. Luke has not yet surfaced from his room, Clinton is going round photographing everywhere in and around the hotel, ready for when they start to decide on sets, and Butch and the kids are playing tennis in the back garden. Ivan is busy on the telephone—I was lucky to catch him—and the wires are humming between England and the U.S.A., and heaven knows where else—incidentally, he'll pay the phone bills, so don't worry. Emma won't be faced with a bill of a few hundred when she gets back.'

Kim smiled. 'He's taken over properly, hasn't he?'

'He always does, love.'

Theodora drifted out to the kitchen, and Kim heard the clatter of crockery. 'Can I help?' she shouted.

'No. Stay there. It's super out here—you should see the view of the sea. I wonder if we can go swimming?'

'We can ask.'

'Mmm, I'd like that.' Theodora came back a few minutes later with two cups of coffee, and sat down. 'Television, I see. Good. There's a film on tonight I'd like to watch. I may let you stop up and watch it too if you're good and have a rest this afternoon.'

'You will? Gosh!'

Theodora laughed. 'All right! I know I sound bossy —but don't forget you shouldn't be here at all.'

'I know. I'm sorry. I'm really very grateful, but I think you already know that.'

'Of course I do, love. I'm only kidding anyway. It's part of the fun. If I hadn't joined Ivan's entourage I might even have ended up as a nurse.'

'You'd have been a good one,' said Kim.

'True.' Theodora smirked modestly. 'Right, lunch, then rest—I'll go and renew old acquaintances and have a long walk. I've bought some fish for us, okay?'

'Lovely.' Kim was hungry.

They ate the grilled fish, then Kim went to bed while Theodora put on a jacket and went to find old friends from the time of the film, and to walk to the village to stock up food for the next few days.

It was quiet, alone in that high-ceilinged apartment with the cool breeze from the sea coming in the open bedroom window. The only sounds were the mewing of gulls and the faint roar of the sea, never-ending and soothing.

Kim slept. When she woke up it was tea time and she could hear the faint voice of a news-reader from the television in the lounge. She crept out to see Theodora curled up on the rug, elbow resting on a leather pouffe, eating a sandwich.

'Hi,' Theodora looked up and waved her free arm. 'Set yourself down, love. Salad sandwich do you?'

'Lovely.'

'Shan't be a minute. I just want to watch the news —I've completely lost touch these last few days, haven't even looked at a newspaper.'

Kim sat down quietly. When the news finished she said: 'I'll get my own sandwiches. You don't have to do——'

'Oh, hush. They're made anyway. I'll pop the kettle on.' Theodora rose and stretched herself. 'Sleep well?'

'Mm, thanks. I feel heaps better. Did you have a good walk?'

'Yes. I was treated like a celebrity in the village store. They recognised me! After this time. Nice people.' Theodora drifted out, laughing. 'The shopkeeper wanted to know if Mr Zolto was coming to visit. I told her no, that he's in the Lake District. They made a packet while he was here—all the film crew, and actors and actresses, and scores of extras—all buying ice creams and fizzy drinks. I must tell him they were asking after him. He likes to be remembered.' She came in again. 'There you are. Eat up.'

An image of Luke came unbidden to Kim's mind. 'I wonder what he's doing?' she said, more to herself.

Theodora gave her a look. She didn't need to ask. 'Still writing, I should imagine,' she answered quietly. She went out again as the kettle began to whistle. Kim began to eat. When Theodora came in with the coffee she sat cross-legged on the rug. 'Are you going back to the Rykin at all?' asked Theodora.

Kim took a deep breath. 'Not while he's there I'm not.'

'What about your car?'

'I've thought about it. I'll leave it there for a while. It won't be in the way.'

'Luke might be there for a while.'

'You mean—while the filming's going on?'

'It's possible—if Ivan wants him to do the film script.'

'Then I'll think of something.' Kim shook her head. 'It doesn't seem important at the moment. I can manage without it in London for a time.'

'Of course you can—and I shouldn't bother you with small details like that. The most important thing is to get you strong again.' Theodora yawned. 'Heavens! I could do with an early night myself.'

'What time's the film on?'

'About nine twenty-five, till eleven.'

'*That's* an early night,' Kim grinned, 'after what we've been having.'

'True. Admittedly you soon get used to less sleep when you're near to Ivan for any length of time—but this sea air just knocks me out. Come on, how do you fancy a quiet walk round the castle? It's closed to the public at five, so we'll not see anyone. Then feet up, a drink, and watch telly.'

'Lovely. I need a bit of exercise. I'm getting dreadfully lazy.'

They cleared away the pots, put the fireguard in front of the fire, and set off to look round the rest of the huge castle. The rooms were beautiful, and there was a haunting quality to the whole place, a quiet and a stillness that gave Kim the strange sensation that if she turned suddenly, she might capture a trace of what had once been. There had been many lives, many loves in this place, and an imprint of them in the very walls, in the air. They trod a corridor in stone, and at the end was a narrow window looking out over the rocks to the sea. Kim caught her breath. 'I can almost smell the past,' she whispered, fearful lest her voice disturb the atmosphere.

'Yes, I know. It's all here. Makes you feel very small and unimportant, doesn't it?' Theodora touched the smooth stone of the window embrasure. 'People have looked out of this window, hundreds of years ago, and seen those same rocks. Perhaps they thought of the future, and wondered how long the castle would stand, who knows?'

The tears trickled down Kim's cheeks. Life was strange, and in a way, all of life was here, captured for

ever in a view from a window. Theodora glanced at her.
'Come on,' she said quietly. 'Let me show you another
part. There's a spiral staircase leading up to the roof.
We'll go there, have a look round, and then go back to
the apartment. We can see the rest of the castle another
day.'

Kim allowed herself to be led away, like a child. An
unutterable sadness had come over her. She could not
have told it to anybody. She loved Luke, and she ached
for him, and she knew it was all too late, much too
late....

Later that evening, when the soft darkness had fallen,
and the television was on, and she had a glass of wine
by her side, she felt less sad. The film was about to
start, and it was one she had seen before, and had
thought superb; funny and sad and tender, *The Apartment*,
with Jack Lemmon and Shirley MacLaine. She
took a look at Theodora, comfortably curled up on a
chair with cigarette and glass of wine, and she smiled.
Theodora was surely one of the kindest, most tactful
people she had ever met. She never pried, never asked
questions, yet she was there if needed, a good listener,
efficient and brisk if necessary.

The telephone shrilled, and Theodora said: 'Oh,
*damn*!'

'I'll answer it,' said Kim, and put down her glass.

'No. It might be Ivan. Stay there, love, I'll get it.'
Theodora went out. She was gone a long time. The film
had well begun when she returned, and glanced at

Kim. 'Only Clinton,' she said, and seated herself. Kim looked at her. There was something wrong. She suddenly felt apprehensive—but she didn't know why.

'Thea? What is it?' she asked.

# CHAPTER TEN

THEODORA looked up, as if miles away. 'What? Oh—nothing! Hey, look at *that*! Doesn't Jack Lemmon make you want to cry and laugh at the same time? What an actor!' She sighed. 'I met him once, at a party. He was *charming*.' She finished her drink. 'Want some more?'

'No, thanks, I've enough here.'

Theodora poured herself a half glassful. 'Cheers.' But she didn't quite look at Kim as she said it. 'Are you stopping until the end of this? You have seen it before?'

'Twice. I feel a little tired. If I can't, I'll just slip off quietly. You won't mind, will you?'

'Course not. Just go when you want.' Theodora sighed and sat back. There were no more words spoken for quite a while after that, and the film took over. But Kim was uneasy. She had no reason to be. She put it down to her illness, to the journey, to general tiredness—it was no use. She couldn't watch it any more. Nothing was registering. The whole atmosphere in the room was wrong, and she didn't know what to do about it.

She stood up quietly. 'If you don't mind, I think I'll go to bed and read for a bit, Thea,' she said.

'Fine. I'll pop in later, see if you need anything.'

'Thanks.' She went quietly out and into her bedroom. Inside she stood for a moment before going over to her window, and looking out at the dark sea pounding restlessly against the rocks. Her heart ached, and her throat was dry with unshed tears. A high clear moon lent an eerie beauty to the scene, and she knew a sense of loneliness that was almost overwhelming. She wanted Luke to be there with her, looking out with her, his arms around her, seeing that beauty and sharing it with her. And it would never be. Never. Their paths had crossed briefly again, and parted. She looked up at the moon, remote, cold, and knew that he could be looking at it too, many miles away. Perhaps he was. A cloud briefly obscured the face of it, and she turned away from the window and began to undress.

She lay in bed, unable to sleep, and there came a tap at the door some time later, and Theodora popped her head in. 'Everything okay?' she whispered.

'Fine. I'm nearly asleep,' Kim lied.

'Good. See you in the morning. Sleep well.'

'I will. Goodnight, Thea.'

'G'night, Kim.' The door was softly closed. She was alone again. And gradually, as she listened to that distant roar of the sea, she was lulled into a state of half sleepiness, not awake, not asleep, but nearly so. She seemed to hear, as from a long distance away, a bell ringing briefly, but it could have been an imagined sound. She could also hear the distant voices from the television, but not loudly enough to disturb her. She drifted deeper down into sleep, and was still. She slept the sleep of utter exhaustion. And when she awoke, it was morning.

The sun streamed in across the carpet and Kim sat up in bed and remembered how depressed she had been, and vowed not to let it happen again. She felt better and she felt stronger. She had no idea of the time because she had forgotten to wind her watch, and it had stopped.

She went to the bathroom and peeped in at the lounge clock, which showed eight o'clock. She would make Theodora a cup of coffee and some toast, and take it in to her. It was the least she could do. She flung open the kitchen window as she waited for the toast to pop up. It was going to be a glorious day. They would go for a walk along the beach, and if Theodora wanted her swim, she could have that too. Humming a little tune, Kim buttered the toast, made the coffee, and took it in.

'Good morning, Thea,' she said, putting the food down.

'Good grief,' was Theodora's sleepy reply. Then: 'Oh! You're awake!'

'I hope so! I don't usually make coffee in my sleep.' Kim sat on the bed. 'I thought I'd surprise you.'

Theodora sat up. She wore an eye-catching red flannelette nightie with high neck and long sleeves, and looked very old-fashioned and very young. 'You've done that, all right. Mmm, toast. Lovely!' She smiled brightly at Kim, and suddenly all Kim's doubts of the previous evening came rushing back. She watched Theodora eating the toast. It was all wrong. Something was all wrong, and she couldn't stand it. Was Theodora regretting coming away?

'Thea,' she said miserably, 'please tell me—*please*. Something's not right, and I don't know what it is——'

'Oh, love, don't!' Theodora put the plate down. 'Don't look so worried. I can't explain—please——'

'There is something——' Kim's breath caught in her throat. 'I can't bear if if you don't tell me. Are you sorry you brought me here? Is that it?'

'No, of course not.' Theodora shook her head. 'It's no use, you've got to know. That phone call—you remember, just as the film was beginning?'

'Yes?' Kim's apprehension grew. That was when the atmosphere had changed.

'It was Clinton. But it was to tell me what had happened. 'He—Luke, I mean, had been writing all day. They'd taken his meals up, right?'

'Yes—and——'

'Well, he came down about nine—and he wanted to know where we were. He'd seen us leaving, apparently, and thought we were going out for the day—you know, for a ride. Then he'd gone into your room and seen the bed stripped—and realised you'd left.' She closed her eyes. 'So he went down and saw Butch—unfortunately.' She stopped.

'Oh, my God! Why unfortunately?'

'Because Butch told him you'd left, and weren't coming back—and Luke asked where had you gone, and Butch said something to the effect that he had no intention of telling Luke, nor had anyone else, and if he didn't like it he could lump it, because as far as he, Butch, was concerned, Luke could go and take a run-

ning jump at himself——' Theodora paused, and gave
a wry grin. 'You've got to hand it to Butch, he knows
how to put it bluntly when he wants. and he more or
less added—don't forget, this was Clinton telling me,
which makes it second-hand—that Luke got right up
his nose and always would do—and to cut a long story
short, Luke then took a swing at Butch and Butch gave
him a black eye!'

'Oh!' There was nothing else Kim could say.

'The story is not yet finished.' Theodora took a deep
swallow of coffee. 'Ah, that's better. Luke marched into
Ivan—fortunately he was at the cottage—I mean,
imagine the guests' reaction if they'd seen this! And
Clinton and Zara were there, and Luke said to Ivan:
"Are you going to tell me where Thea has gone with
Kim or not?" to which Ivan's reply was apparently no,
because he thought it better all round you should get
away for a few days, you weren't well, etcetera—Ivan
can bring tears to the eyes of the strongest man if he
chooses and I can imagine him laying it on thick—to
which Luke's reply was, in Clinton's words, and he was
there, and he has a perfect memory: 'I intend to find
out one way or another, and it will save a lot of trouble
if you tell me now." So Ivan waffled on a bit—and
Luke said: "Take your choice. I'll give you ten minutes
to decide. I'm going up to my room for the manuscript
and if you don't want to see it burnt in the fireplace,
you'll tell me." And he marched out.

'Clinton looked at Ivan, who looked at Zara—who
hadn't said a word so far, and she then said: "He means
it." Then Luke came back, carrying his papers, walked

over to the fireplace, took out a box of matches, and said: "Well, are you going to tell me or not?"' Theodora paused to drink more coffee. 'Now, picture the scene. There's Ivan, who, let's face it, wants that book for a film—out of which he intends to make a few more million, give or take a thousand or so, and there's Luke, with his eye going nicely rainbow-coloured, and Clinton, and Zara, and Butch, who had come in to look after Ivan—as if he needs it—and Luke definitely means what he says.'

'So?' Kim's eyes were wide.

'So—Ivan told him.'

'Oh.' She felt weak. 'Do you think—do you think —he intends to c-come up here?'

The answer was surprising. Theodora shook her head gently. 'No,' she said.

'But—but he insisted on getting the address——' Kim was totally bewildered.

Theodora's next words were even more startling. 'He doesn't intend to, my love—he's already *here*.'

'What?' Ashen-faced, Kim stared at her.

She nodded. 'He arrived last night. He came at the end of the film. Now you know why I was on pins after that phone call. I couldn't tell you. I wanted you off to bed—and fortunately, you went. Because I was going to play *hell* with him. That's why Clinton phoned me, to warn me. Boy, was I ready for him!'

'I heard a bell——'

'That was him, arriving.'

'Where is he?' asked Kim.

'Asleep—I hope—in the other bedroom.' Theodora

smiled. 'And has he got a *glorious* black eye! He very nearly got another from me.' Her eyes sparkled. 'I decided that when he came in I would have no nonsense at all. Apparently he'd set off in a flaming temper. I was prepared for battle. And Kim, you've never seen me in a temper, have you? The doorbell rang, I opened the door, I let him in the hall—I'd shut the other door to the lounge so I knew you wouldn't hear, and I told him exactly what I thought of him. Oh, boy, did I tell *him*!' She closed her eyes briefly. 'Then when I'd finished I waited for him to blow up—and I was ready for anything—except what happened.'

'What—happened?'

'He looked at me, and he said, very quietly—which made me feel, of course, as though I'd been screaming like a fishwife: "I'm sorry, Thea, you have every right to bawl me out, and I didn't expect any different—but nothing would have stopped me coming." It took the wind right out of my sails, I can tell you that. Then he added very quietly: "Can I have a cup of coffee?"'

'And then what——?'

'I brought him in the lounge and made him one. He followed me out to the kitchen and watched me make it, and I looked at him, and thought I'd never seen a man who looked so unhappy. And then—we talked.' She stopped.

Kim couldn't say a word. She looked numbly at Theodora, waiting for she knew not what. The silence stretched until it was almost at breaking point, then: 'We talked for a couple of hours. Or rather he talked, and I listened.' Theodora looked at Kim, and there were tears glinting in her eyes. 'And listen, love—he wants to talk to you.'

'Oh, but——' Kim clasped her hands together. 'Don't you see what will happen? It'll start all over again, and I can't—I just can't take any more——'

'Wait, listen to me for a minute. *I* told him precisely the same thing—and he said, no—it wouldn't be like that at all, and I said, oh yes, but I've seen you two together and watched the sparks fly and I'm here to look after Kim, thank you very much, and I'm going to do just that—and he said—do you know what he said?' Kim shook her head. 'He said, "I swear I only want to talk, not to upset her, and one way or another I'm going to, and no one, not even you, Thea, is going to stop me —but," he said, "I swear to you on my life that I won't touch her or go near her, that I won't shout or get angry".'

'He might have meant it when he told you, but he's different when he's alone——'

And Luke's voice from the doorway, effectively silencing her: 'I give you my word.'

They both looked round. He stood there, lean, dark, unshaven, his face pale and drawn, and with a beautiful black eye. Kim rose to her feet.

'I don't want to talk to you,' she said.

'Please, Kim.' Their eyes met across the room. A pulse beat in her throat. She had never seen him like that before. He didn't look intimidating, he looked like a man who had come to the end of a long journey, and was exhausted. 'I'll wait in the lounge,' he said. 'And I'll keep on waiting until you will talk—and I don't care how long it takes.' He walked out and closed the door after him.

Kim looked at Theodora. 'What do I do now?'

'Go and get washed and dressed, then go in and see him. You heard what he said. He'll wait until you do. And he means that too.' Theodora lay back, pulled the covers up to her face. 'I'm staying here,' she said. 'Let me know when it's all over.' And she turned away and closed her eyes.

Kim went out of the room, and Luke was standing by the lounge window looking out. He turned when he heard her footsteps, turned and looked at her. 'It's no use,' she said. 'It's all been said already. I don't know what you hoped to achieve by following me here, but I'm not strong enough at the moment to let you tear me apart. It was over three years ago.'

'Yes, that's what I thought. And now I know I was wrong.'

'Wrong? About Paul, you mean? It took you long enough to find out!'

'I don't care about Paul. I don't care if you did have an affair——'

'I didn't,' she said flatly. 'He'd "arranged" it. He was jealous. But you believed him, not me. You made your choice then.'

He moved away from the window, towards her. 'Don't come any nearer,' she said. 'You promised.'

He stood still. 'Yes. I wasn't going to—touch you. I wanted to talk nearer——'

'You're near enough. I can see you and hear you, that's near enough. Don't you think I've had enough?

I adjusted my life three years ago, I didn't forget you because I couldn't, but I learned to adjust. I didn't know you'd be at the Rykin. If I had I wouldn't have gone, I promise you that.'

She turned away and began to walk to her own bedroom. 'I'm going to get dressed. If you want to leave that's fine by me. You can't hurt me any more than you have done, whatever you do or say now.'

His voice halted her; it was very harsh, as if he were under a great strain. 'If I said that I loved you, would that hurt?'

She turned. 'Love? You don't know the meaning of the word.'

'I've always loved you, and I always will. There's a very fine dividing line between love and hate. I thought I hated you, but now I know I was wrong. I love you so much it hurts. I love you so much that it tears me apart—and I'm telling you now because there's nothing left for me. Nothing else. You can say what you like—you can laugh if you want, it won't alter my feelings. God knows I've tried to stop loving you—and it doesn't work. I've lived with your face, haunting me, for the past three years. Seeing you was like seeing a ghost. I tried to exorcise it if you like, by what I did. I made love to you out of desperation, hating, loving, all at the same time—and the force and power of my feelings was shattering.' He looked at her, and she saw the pain she had seen before in his eyes.

'Then you played that record. Do you know why I walked out of the room when you played it? I'll tell you—and you can have a good laugh if you like. I left

the room because if I'd stayed I would have wept, and
a grown man doesn't cry; it's not done. I went to my
room, and I stood at the window and I couldn't see a
damned thing, because everything had gone blurred.
That's funny, isn't it?' He paused. 'Why aren't you
laughing?' He rubbed his hand across his face. 'Then
I went down and took the dog out.'

Kim walked slowly towards him. When she was a
yard or so away, she stopped. 'I wanted to hurt you,'
she said. 'I wanted very much to punish you—but if I
could have stopped it, at the last moment, I would have.
Because I hurt myself far more.'

They stood, only a few feet apart, not reaching out,
not touching, because they couldn't. The gulf was too
wide. It yawned between them, and it stretched over
the years, and there was no way for either of them to
breach it, because the pain, the scars, were too vivid
and raw.

'It's no use,' she said gently. 'Don't you see? What's
done is done. You say you love me, but if that's love,
life is better without it. It's all pain and anguish. We
may not be able to live apart, but we could never live
together. We'd destroy each other.'

They looked into each other's eyes, and they didn't
speak. The room was filled with an unbearable tension.
It filled Kim too. The pain was in her, and she longed
to weep, to have the release of tears, but she held them
back. 'I love you,' she said. 'And I've never stopped
either, and I wish I could. Don't you see,' she cried in
anguish, 'we're no good for each other?'

'Yes, I see,' he said very quietly. 'But I had to come

here. I had to. Nothing would have stopped me coming.
But now I shall leave. I shan't go back to the Rykin, it
holds too many painful memories. But Ivan shall have
his book, and the film will be made. When you and
Thea are finished here, you can go back there. I shall
have gone.' He picked up his jacket from the chair.
'Say goodbye to Thea for me.' And he walked out of
the door and closed it behind him.

She would never see him again. Kim knew it the
moment he walked out into the hall. Then she heard
the outer door open, and then that too closed. She
stood there silently, knowing Luke was at last walking
out of her life for ever. And she knew she couldn't let
it happen. In a blinding flash of realisation, she knew
why.

She ran to the door, opened it, into the hall, opened
the front door and looked out. He was walking down the
stone corridor.

'Luke,' she called, 'wait!' He turned, he looked, and
as she walked towards him, he began to walk back towards her. As she reached him, she put out her arms
to him and touched him, and held him.

'Don't go,' she said. 'Please don't go.'

He looked down at her, then he smiled. He put his
arms round her, bent his head and kissed her. She felt
the tears on her face, and she didn't know whose they
were, and it didn't matter any more. They clung to
each other, then he picked her up and carried her back
into the hall and closed the door, putting her down as
he did so.

'Don't ever go,' she said. 'I can't live without you. I

love you, my darling, more than anything else in the world.' Then she was crying, and laughing at the same time, and he was laughing with her, holding her as if he would never let her go, ever again.

'It's going to be all right,' he whispered. 'Now it's going to be all right. I know it now.' And he picked her up again as if she was as light as a feather, and carried her through the lounge, and into her bedroom. Then he closed the door very firmly behind him.

# Take these 4 best-selling novels FREE

# Harlequin Presents...

## Take these 4 best-selling novels FREE

That's right! FOUR first-rate Harlequin romance novels by four world renowned authors, FREE, as your introduction to the Harlequin Presents Subscription Plan. Be swept along by these FOUR exciting, poignant and sophisticated novels . . . . Travel to the Mediterranean island of Cyprus in **Anne Hampson**'s "Gates of Steel" . . . to Portugal for **Anne Mather**'s "Sweet Revenge" . . . to France and **Violet Winspear**'s "Devil in a Silver Room" . . . and the sprawling state of Texas for **Janet Dalley**'s "No Quarter Asked."

Join the millions of avid Harlequin readers all over the world who delight in the magic of a really exciting novel. SIX great NEW titles published EACH MONTH! Each month you will get to know exciting, interesting, true-to-life people . . . . You'll be swept to distant lands you've dreamed of visiting . . . . Intrigue, adventure, romance, and the destiny of many lives will thrill you through each Harlequin Presents novel.

 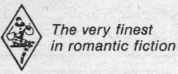

# Harlequin Presents...

### The very finest in romantic fiction

**Get all the latest books before they're sold out!**

As a Harlequin subscriber you actually receive your personal copies of the latest Presents novels immediately after they come off the press, so you're sure of getting all 6 each month.

**Cancel your subscription whenever you wish!**

You don't have to buy any minimum number of books. Whenever you decide to stop your subscription just let us know and we'll cancel all further shipments.

**Your FREE gift includes**

*Sweet Revenge* by **Anne Mather**
*Devil in a Silver Room* by **Violet Winspear**
*Gates of Steel* by **Anne Hampson**
*No Quarter Asked* by **Janet Dailey**

# FREE Gift Certificate
## and subscription reservation

**Mail this coupon today!**

In U.S.A.:
Harlequin Reader Service
MPO Box 707
Niagara Falls, NY 14302

In Canada:
Harlequin Reader Service
649 Ontario Street
Stratford, Ontario
N5A 6W4

**Harlequin Reader Service:**

Please send me my 4 Harlequin Presents books free. Also, reserve a subscription to the 6 new Harlequin Presents novels published each month. Each month I will receive 6 new Presents novels at the low price of $1.50 each [*Total - $9.00 per month*]. There are no shipping and handling or any other hidden charges. I am free to cancel at any time, but even if I do, these first 4 books are still mine to keep absolutely FREE without any obligation.

NAME                    (PLEASE PRINT)

ADDRESS

CITY          STATE / PROV      ZIP / POSTAL CODE

Offer expires June 30, 1980          00356416000
Offer not valid to present subscribers

# What readers say about Harlequin Romances

"Harlequins take away the world's troubles and for a while you can live in a world of your own where love reigns supreme."
L.S.,* Beltsville, Maryland

"Thank you for bringing romance back to me."
J.W., Tehachapi, California

"I find Harlequins are the only stories on the market that give me a satisfying romance with sufficient depth without being maudlin."
C.S., Bangor, Maine

"Harlequins are magic carpets...away from pain and depression...away to other people and other countries one might never know otherwise."
H.R., Akron, Ohio

*Names available on request